From Hay to Eternity

From Hay to Eternity

Ten Devilish Tales of Crime and Deception

Sandra Murphy

White City Press

Contents

Copyright

dialogue and events in this book are wholly fictional, and any resemblance to companies and actual persons, living or dead, is coincidental.

Superstition

I lived a life of caution and sanity, friends laughing at the oddity of my superstitions.

Step on a crack, break your mother's back. A black cat crossing your path is bad luck, just like walking under a ladder. Three black birds mean death. Damn birds. A penny, found face up, good luck; face down, bad. Spilling salt definitely bad luck, countered by throwing it over your left shoulder.

I found it impossible to separate belief from coincidence—how much is real and how much only imagination following the silliness of my mind?

I'd avoided cracks, cats and ladders, studied fallen pennies before picking up or passing by, flung salt before the bad luck could get me, for all the good it did.

That last day, I went out early to search the yard and bushes for the paper, as always. Heading back to the porch, to sit and sip coffee, read and lie in filling out the Sudoku, I stopped abruptly, staring at the house. What if, instead of superstition, it was really an omen?

I dropped the paper right there and ran inside.

I pawed through the sensible outfits, all khaki and navy with small, very small, touches of red, until I found the one I was looking for, my guilty secret—a lavender jumpsuit I wore zipped down to show the purple t-shirt underneath, cleavage balanced above. Large silver hoops hung from my ears. I found the purple tennis shoes, dug out makeup to match—purple shadow, three layers of mascara, a plum lipstick.

Then I went out and had ice cream for breakfast.

All day long I did the things I always put off. I test-drove a dark green Mustang convertible, looking like a grape among leaves. I watched a movie that had no redeeming value except it made me laugh. And in spite of the large tub of popcorn, extra butter please, a super-sized soda and a box of Milk Duds, I stopped by the drive-in dive for a foot-long chili cheese dog for supper. I figured, this once, I wouldn't worry about cholesterol or calories.

I wrote out some stories I'd had in mind and felt I'd really brought the characters to life. I wrote instructions for the next day so my best friend would have something concrete to follow. And I tried to explain—there's coincidence, there's luck, there's real and there's imaginary, with no boundaries in-between.

Then there's belief.

Belief when there's no rational explanation. Certainty where there is no evidence. Knowledge that in a pile of superstitions, one or two will really come true, really happen.

So when I got ready for bed, I didn't take a quick shower, but a long bubble bath, candles all around, scented oil floating in iridescent shadows, a glass of white wine balanced on the tub's edge, its flavor a crisp and cold contrast to the warm water.

It was tempting to stay in the tub until the hot water ran out, but I didn't want to look all pruney, so forced myself to dry off, moisturize and put on a nice gown.

Then I climbed into bed, pulled the phone onto my lap and fixed it to forward calls to my best friend. I thought about it for a while and dialed my automated wake-up service. I set it to call at 9 o'clock with this message... "Hi, it's me. Call me as soon as you get this message. If I don't answer, call 9-1-1 and then come over. No need for lights and sirens."

Then I turned out the lamp.

The next morning, as an ambulance coasted to a stop at the curb, three black birds, perched on the porch roof, flew away.

The Chicken Pot Pie Fiasco

Thanksgiving is different at your house than mine. A lot of people have turkey and dressing, others serve ham and cornbread, and some make everybody's favorite food. Here, that means chicken pot pie. There's one big pie, and if there's some of the inside stuff left over, there are little pies for later. I like that part.

This year, it won't be the same. Chris Honey, he's the Dad, went away a while back. Everybody's sad about that. He said, "Duty calls," and had on his uniform so we all knew it was serious stuff.

If you know your geography, which I have to say I don't, we kind of know where he's working. We look at the map on the computer and pretend that on this mountain or by this river, is where we see him. Skype, another thing I don't really understand, lets us talk to him. His buddies wave or make funny faces, and at the end of the call, everybody cries. It's a good thing to be able to see he's really okay like he says.

Packages with books, pictures of the kids, cards,

notes and even food are a big hit. Pringles, the salt and vinegar kind that make my tongue go all tingly, are a favorite, because they aren't smashed up crumbs when the box gets there. I've found out though, you can't mail chicken pot pies, which is part of why everybody's sad.

Bonnie Honey, she's the Mom, tries to be cheerful, but sometimes I hear her crying late at night when she thinks no one else is awake. She walks back and forth in the bedroom until she gets real tired. I try my best to keep her spirits up, but there are days when it's a lot of work.

So, here we are, trying to act like this Thanksgiving is just like any other. We've got pots and pans, bowls and spoons, flour and veggies on every counter in the kitchen. I'm pretty sure there will be enough chicken pot pie inside stuff left for little pies later.

When the phone rang, Bonnie Honey got there first. She nodded a lot, smiled a little, but tried not to, said "Yeah, sure" a bunch of times. Finally she said, "That reminds me, I forgot to get chicken for the pot pies. I'll leave right now!" and she hung up the phone.

"Gotta go, forgot the chicken! Grandma, can you get the vegetables going? I'll be back as soon as I can." With that, she was out the door and running for the car. I noticed that she put on some lipstick and brushed her hair before she backed out of the driveway though.

Ralphie, he's the dog, cute little guy who sheds a puppy's worth of hair a day, was playing with his stuffed toy, the one they call The Chicken. It was slobber-free and fresh out of the dryer, bright yellow with big red lips and giant white teeth. He carries that thing everywhere and gets all panicky if he can't find it. Sometimes I hide it just to watch him run in circles and sniff like a bloodhound. Right now, he was in the kitchen where he could snoopervise but not get stepped on.

I decided to liven things up a little, just a diversion from any sad, you know? I snuck up behind Ralphie and gave him the gentlest little nudge on his backside. He yelped, went straight up in the air, The Chicken went flying and...landed right in the big chicken pot pie cooking pot!

Well, Ralphie saw where it went and started barking like crazy. Grandma was cutting up carrots and missed the whole thing. "Ralphie, hush now. You'll get some with your dinner." She turned around and dumped all the carrots in the pan. "Now where did I put my glasses?" She wandered off to find them.

Aunt Millie came in a few minutes later. Ralphie tried to tell her about The Chicken but she didn't get it either. "Good grief, they haven't even peeled the potatoes yet. They'll never be cooked if they don't go in right now." She peeled a whole bunch of potatoes, some yellow on the inside, some red on the outside and one that was purple! She'd just dumped them in the pot when Twin # 1 and Twin # 2 started to fight. "Ralphie, be quiet. Between you and the kids, I can't hear myself think." She went to find the boys.

Grandma came back and started fussing with more vegetables. I think this time it was green beans. She kept saying fresh beans were better but pulling the strings off them was a pain. Personally, I didn't see any strings, but then I'm not what you could call a cook, although I do love the Food Network. The green beans got chopped into bite-size pieces and into the pot they went.

Aunt Millie came back and reported that Twin #1 and Twin #2 were on time-out, which meant they had to sit quietly and ponder about their manners on a day when everybody is supposed to be thankful for what they have. I suspected they were really pondering about revenge, but maybe that's just what I would do. I never get put on time-out, but that could be because I never get caught. I am stealthy.

Ralphie kept yelling about The Chicken, especially when Grandma said it was time to add the bouillon cubes and chicken broth. I'm pretty sure Ralphie doesn't know what chicken broth is (he doesn't watch the Food Network; he's an Animal Planet guy, except when they show monkeys—then he's a crazy guy), but he barked a lot anyway, especially when Grandma stirred everything up real good.

"Oh, good grief. I've got salted butter. It's supposed to be unsalted," Grandma said. "Ralphie, hush.

I'll be right back. I'm just going downstairs for the right kind of butter."

She wasn't gone long, but it was enough time for Uncle Tim to sneak into the kitchen and find the bag of pearl onions. The recipe said to use a few, but he put in the whole bag! He does like those onions. They look like marbles to me, but mushy.

There was time for Aunt Delores to pop in too. "Doesn't this smell great? I can't wait to get a big spoonful of chicken and lots of crust. It's the best part." She poured in a big bag of frozen peas.

Grandma got back and added the right kind of butter, some flour (she spilled a little on the floor, but we don't say anything when she does that), and some cream. I managed to lick the cup when she turned her back but I was quick and she didn't catch me. The trick to staying in the kitchen during prep (that's what they call it on the Food Network), is to stay out of the way and be quiet. Stealthy.

Grandma stirred everything together and when her spoon hit the big lump that was The Chicken, she said, "I can't believe that girl thinks she forgot to get the chicken for the pot pies. Here's a big ol' piece of chicken right here. She must've put it in and forgot. Well, Ralphie, we'd better cut it up in tiny pieces so it's easier to chew."

Well, you can guess, Ralphie went nutso barking when he saw the knife headed for the pot! Ralphie got a time-out too—out in the yard, that is. While

Grandma escorted him out the door—that means pulled him along by his collar because he stiffened up his legs, and she couldn't make him go out (he watches *Law and Order* and he has rights)—Grandma kept right on walking. She acted like she couldn't understand what he was talking about and said, "What? You want to sit out in the sunshine all by yourself? Okay."

While she was outside dealing with Ralphie, Aunt Millie showed up again. She dumped a lot of the chicken pot pie inside stuff that included The Chicken in the baking dish and put a crust on top. She stabbed the crust a few times, "to let out the steam," she said, and luckily, she missed stabbing The Chicken. Into the oven it went, one hour at 375 degrees, if you care about that kind of thing.

Now considering Bonnie Honey just went to pick up chicken at the store, she was gone a long time. The chicken pot pie got done cooking, cooled off a little and everybody was getting worried, not to mention hungry, when we finally heard the car in the driveway.

Bonnie Honey rushed in and she was *not* carrying any chicken, let me tell you! She didn't even have a grocery bag. She saw everybody at the table, all waiting for her and said, "I've got a surprise for you. Close your eyes and no peeking." If you looked close, and I did, you could see her face was all pinkish.

Everybody closed their eyes, even me, although

mine may have been open just a slit, which as you know, doesn't really count except in hide and seek. On account of that slit, I got to see the surprise first.

When Bonnie Honey yelled, "Open your eyes," everybody did, and then Grandma cried, Aunt Millie kept patting her chest, and Twin #1 and Twin #2 jumped up and down and yelled. Nobody gave them a time-out because the surprise was Chris Honey was home for Thanksgiving and chicken pot pie.

Everybody talked a lot and all at the same time so things got confusing for a while, but nobody cared about that. Finally, as I was about to faint from hunger, Grandma said, "Let's eat," just as Chris Honey asked where Ralphie was.

"Oh my, he's on time-out in the yard. I forgot," Grandma said. She sent Twin #1 to bring him in. The barking started all over again, but since it was welcome-home barking, he didn't get in trouble.

After all that, everybody sat down and got ready to eat, napkins on laps, forks in hand. Chris Honey got to do the honors as they call it, which means he got to cut into the crust first and serve everybody else. He was pretty surprised when he did, because there was a big squeaky noise! Ralphie had a fit because he recognized The Chicken's squeaker. I took the opportunity to mosey back into the kitchen. They didn't even see me leave the dining room. I never get caught. Stealthy.

I could still hear what was going on though.

There were more squeaks and a few "What the heck is that?" comments. After a while, a very indignant Ralphie came into the kitchen and laid The Chicken on the dog bed. The Chicken was covered in chicken pot pie inside stuff so Ralphie licked and licked until he cleaned it all off.

In the dining room, everybody just stared at the big chicken pot pie. "Should we eat it? It has dog germs from The Chicken," said Aunt Millie.

"It doesn't have any chicken in it. Is it still a chicken pot pie?" asked Twin #2.

"How many dog germs do you think are in there?" That was Uncle Tim. He wanted those pearl onions.

"TEN!" Twin #1 says if you say anything like you know what you're talking about, people will believe you.

"Ten germs? Are you positive?" Grandma didn't sound sure.

"Yes, and we are all immune since Ralphie kisses us every day. Besides, The Chicken just had a bath in the washer."

Grandma thought that over for a minute and then said, "I think you're right. Let's eat!" and so they did.

Since their attention was elsewhere, I thought it was a good time for me to eat too. Twin #2, who's nosy and a tattletale, saw me. "Grandma, Louie's eating chicken pot pie inside stuff out of the pan on the stove!"

*

I, Louie, the one who never gets caught, had the evidence all around my mouth. I'm now on my very first time-out, which is why I could tell you about Thanksgiving at our house and how to make a chicken pot pie.

It's time for my nap. When I wake up, I have to practice sneakiness. I want to make sure this will be my *only* time-out.

Stealthy.

Signed,

Louie the Cat

The Space Heater vs. the Window Fan

For the fifth time in a month, I booted up the computer to find a cheery message—"Welcome! Follow this simple tutorial to install your high speed internet connection in just minutes!" The tutorial is neither simple nor fast. It *always* requires a call to tech support and that takes from thirty to sixty-one minutes. Today we set a speed record—only twenty-three!

Machines must have an age-old distrust of me. In a past life, I may have abused one, kicked a furnace, smacked a candy dispenser, or cussed out any number of washers, dryers and/or other helpful aids that just stopped working at the worst possible moment.

Of course, it's not always the appliance's fault. Sometimes it's the power company, like the day the electricity went out as I tried to get dressed for a wedding—my sister's. I'd taken a bath and tried to dry off, but it was so hot that day, the only way to stay dry enough to get dressed was to stand between the fan and air conditioning vent. It had to be at that exact moment we had a brownout, or maybe it was just sun spots. Anyway, I'm fighting to pull on pantyhose, but the skin's getting sweaty faster than I can get the nylon up over my knees, to the hoo-ha and up to my waist. I nearly strangled myself getting a bra on. I slapped on makeup in the dim light and hoped for the best. I threw extra makeup in my purse in case I had to do it all over again in the car. Full face makeup in the tiny rearview mirror is not a good look, trust me. The photographer refused to let me stand in the back row—apparently, it's a given the maid of honor is guaranteed a front row spot. Let's just say the camera hated me too.

Then there was the day the washer went to cold water only and the dryer took the pledge against warm air, I went to the number one laundromat in town. They must have bribed everyone they knew to get that title because the machines were so old, I couldn't even read the buttons to start the process. Although I was guaranteed really dry clothes for only 50 cents, everything was just short of wet and a step away from damp and I was out of time. I couldn't find a restroom—really, no bathroom for people who are trapped here for a couple of hours?— so I changed clothes in the car while parked in the supermarket parking lot. In retrospect, it might have been a better choice to park somewhere besides in the first row off a major street.

This is just to show I have a history of bad luck with machines of all sorts, so it was no surprise to me, when one day I cussed at them and they started to talk back. First it was the car that didn't want to start. I raised my voice and gave my perfectly valid opinion that it had gas and what did it want from me, I had to go, I was late. Clear as the bell that warns "Door open.", I heard, "What? It would kill you to change the oil once in a while? They don't put those stickers on my windshield for decoration you know."

Now some people might say I was a little delusional that day, but I know I was perfectly sober. Who can afford to be otherwise given the repair bills I have? I was in my right mind, too, as best as I can determine anyway. Besides, everybody's a little crazy, right? Back to the computer and its forgetful modem.

When the modem finally rebooted and I got online, up popped a little note that said the space heater I have—the one guaranteed not to fall over, start a fire and kill me dead—is defective and could I please send it back to the company who will of course, reimburse me for the shipping and the price of the item, minus use, as determined by some obscure formula only the company engineer knows, and it has to be in the same packaging as it came in, okay? Well, sure, as soon as I pry three cats out of the box who seem to think the box is their own personal futon or something and then try to find the Styrofoam chunks I had to take out of the box so three cats fit in there.

I managed all that, but could not get the damn space heater back in the box. I swear it must have watched me try to get a cat in a crate for a trip to the vet. The cats have all learned if they go spread-eagled there's no way to get all four legs in the door at once. Claws hang on with a death grip to the opening, the door, my clothes and me until I either give up or tell them I've thought of a way to explain to the vet why they have four broken legs. I didn't think the space heater would be impressed by a vet threat.

I fought with the heater for a while and then the voice came. "Why are you sending me away? I've been good."

Without thinking, I said, "You've been recalled. There's a defect in your computer brain and you have to be reprogrammed—otherwise you're a danger to yourself and others, namely me." What the hell? I'm talking to a space heater. Does that make me a space cadet?

"NO! I won't go! There's nothing wrong with me, let me stay. The fan gets to stay and he runs all the time. I have to sit here, months out of the year, doing nothing. It's boring, but do I complain? I do not. I wait until you're cold and I warm up the whole room. Is this the thanks I get?"

"The fan circulates the warm air from the furnace vent in the winter and the cold air from the a/c in the hot weather," I said. "You're a one season kind of guy. I'm sorry, but this has to be done for both our sakes."

I gave up on the heater going back in the box and carried them both downstairs and to the back door. It was the same fight to get out the door as it was to get it in the box. I finally managed and the thing got heavier and heavier as I walked across the yard. Then it started to get hot. I was afraid to set it down, but couldn't hold it either while I unlocked the gate. The Dumpster sits right outside the fence, so with one big heave, I pitched the thing up and over. "This is the only way. If you didn't fight me on this, you could have gone home and been rehabbed, but now it's the trash bin for you!"

I didn't quite get the heater over the fence, or maybe it used the electrical cord to save itself, because the plug got caught between the fence boards, and the heater hung on for dear life. Sparks flew from the plug and began to smolder on the wood. "You stop that right now! The message said you were dangerous and now you're just proving it."

There was no reply, but more sparks flew and the dry grass started to sizzle. The wooden fence went beyond smoldering and into flames. I grabbed my cell phone to call for help, but no signal. How could I not have any bars in my own back yard? I redialed, held it to my ear and hoped to hear, "9-1-1, what's your emergency?" but all I heard was, "The space heater is my friend. He keeps me company when I'm on the charger."

I heard the storm door bang open behind me. "Stay in the house," I yelled. It had to be the dog—the cats aren't strong enough to open the door alone, and not organized enough to work together. A strong wind blew up and the flames retreated. The fence showed no damage, although moments before, it had shown char marks. I could hear the leaves on the tree next door beat against each other as the force of the wind picked up. "Get out and stay out!" said a voice I didn't know. "I can take care of this house by myself. You're not needed."

I turned and had to brush the hair out of my eyes. The tug of the wind on my clothes was a pull now. The window fan stood in the open doorway, the speed turned up faster than the old standards of low, medium, high I knew and used. With a final sputter, the space heater fell from the fence to land on top of the Dumpster. "Go, toss him in the trash bin now, while he's weak. He won't be able to regain his strength before the trash truck comes."

I unlocked the gate. The space heater was cool to the touch, unlike our trip through the yard. I opened the lid of the Dumpster and toppled him in. "I'm so sorry," I said. "I wish things could have been different." I dropped the lid.

The wind had died down. I closed and locked the gate, checked my cell phone—four bars and a text that said, "I'm sorry."

I gave it a pat and replied, "You're forgiven. Just don't let it happen again." It might be time for an upgrade, but I'm sure not going to say anything ahead of time. I looked up at the second-floor window. There sat the window fan, doing what he always does—making sure I'm safe and comfortable.

On days when it feels like everybody and everything is out to get you, it's good to know you've got at least one friend.

Waffling on Cherokee Street

"Where are you?" Bernice came down the stairs with Ozzie, the Westie-ish dog. "How can he get lost, Ozzie?"

"I went to get a drink of water. I got parched, waiting on the porch," said Ken. "Let's go, no slowing down. We don't want the girls to be mad at Ozzie because he was late. They might give him a Mohawk or something."

"Ozzie, Ken's just being silly. Let's go."

Once they were all buckled in, Ken backed out of the driveway and headed for Cherokee Street. "Do you want to eat an early lunch while Ozzie gets groomed?" Ken was always in the mood for an early lunch—and a late one besides.

"I think I'll walk around to see the new shops. Gladys said there's a new resale store that's good. Who knows what else is there now? It's been a couple of months since we were down that way."

"Do you have your cane? I don't want to find you

laid out on the sidewalk again," Ken said. "We were late for brunch."

"You were just upset about that nice man who helped me until you got there. Such a beautiful accent," said Bernice. "He treated us at his restaurant so what are you complaining about? I should write to the mayor and ask him to fix all the uneven sidewalks."

"You get right on that. It was a good meal. Taquerias know what they're doing. If you're going to fall down again, make it in front of a restaurant."

"Just watch the traffic and get us there in one piece."

Ozzie woofed his agreement.

*

"Got your cane?"

"It's mostly for decoration," said Bernice. "If I were a man, I'd be dashing. Now I just look like an old lady who can't walk straight."

"If you were a man, I wouldn't look twice at you, dashing or not. I think it makes you look elegant. It goes with the purple tennis shoes."

"Why, thank you. Ozzie's new haircut will make him elegant too."

There was the usual barkfest and a race around the shop when Ozzie entered the Woof and Wash, but everyone was soon untangled. Bernice patted Ozzie on the head, told him to be a good boy and headed out to window shop.

The first store had lava lamps. Bernice wondered how they worked. Sadly, the bright yellow, neon lime and citrus orange colors of her younger years were now retro. Bernice thought retro should smell like mothballs, but this place reeked of patchouli and made her sneeze.

Down the block, Bernice saw a resale shop with furniture, somewhere to take a discreet rest while "testing" out a chair or two. "Don't forget, old girl," she reminded herself, "no sofas. The last time it took two people to get you out of that old couch with no springs. There should have been a sign on it."

After three chairs were tested and Bernice refreshed, she crossed the street to find a bonanza—a bead store! Bernice loved the bright colors, odd shapes, textures and possibilities beads presented.

"Hello?"

"Welcome to my store. I am Paul. I don't believe we've met." The man came from the back room, arms full of bags. "I was just unpacking a new shipment. Would you like to see?"

Bernice would like nothing better. "I have to pick up Ozzie at the Woof and Wash at two o'clock. Until then, I plan on enjoying myself right here."

"I have millefiori, the Italian cane glass beads. The colors are so bright. Here are lampwork beads—a pink piggy, funny fish and frogs with lips, birds of all colors. The penguins are resin, but little girls love them for pins and necklaces. And, of course, crystals."

"How much are pink piggies? I love the birds too...oh, there are cats and a dog;it almost looks like Ozzie."

"Why don't you just pick what you like and I'll make a price? It does my heart good to meet someone who is as enthusiastic about beads as I am," said Paul.

"Paul, you may regret saying that. If it was up to me, I'd own every bead in this store."

"Then let us begin." As Paul glanced out the window, his smile faltered, just for a second. Bernice turned to see what startled him and saw a black car with tinted windows pass by. "We'll save the crystals for last, shall we?"

The hour passed quickly. Bernice had to make her final decisions so she could get back to the Woof and Wash before Ozzie got himself dirty. Last time he'd played with a Spaniel while he waited and almost had to have another bath.

"I'd better see if Ken's back. Figure up how much I owe you, okay?" Bernice walked to the front of the store to look for their car. She'd limited herself to one bag since Ken got kind of sensitive about that kind of thing. Geez, she'd only asked him to build a few shelves. Well, floor to eye level was only a few, right? "Yes, he's bringing Ozzie out. I'd better hurry."

"Just sign here. I put in a special treat as well. I do hope we meet again, Bernice. I've had such an enjoyable afternoon."

"As have I, Paul." Something about him made more formal speech sound right. Elegant, Bernice decided, he's elegant. Maybe dashing, too.

When Bernice left the shop, she carried something she didn't count on—a threat to her life.

*

"Did you notice a black car back there?" Bernice thought she saw it but coming out of the shop into the sunlight, it took a minute for her eyes to adjust and then the car was gone.

"What car? I'm hungry." Of course, Ken's brain was in his stomach as usual. "I found some cool old nails at the hardware store. I'll pop the trunk so you can put your bag inside while I buckle Ozzie's seat belt."

Once Bernice was settled in the car, Ken's mind turned to, what else, food. "Did you find a spot for lunch?"

"I did. It's a waffle place."

"I don't want breakfast. I'm hungrier than that," said Ken. "Maybe barbeque or, I don't know, something more substantial."

"This place has got what you want. There's a menu on the door and I saw they serve everything on waffles. There was one with barbequed pulled pork and coleslaw, one with mac and cheese and they have slider waffles..." Ken had a weakness for sliders, the St. Louis favorite of chili, cheddar cheese and fried eggs and sometimes a hamburger patty or two.

"Which way?"

"Turn right at the next stop sign," Bernice said. "Ozzie, hang on."

Ozzie braced himself just in time. Ken took the turn almost on two wheels. In no time flat, they were headed for a waffle lunch.

*

"Now that was a great meal," said Ken. "I'll get the car and come back for you and Ozzie. He might need a tree break."

Ozzie did, and led the way to the nearest tree. Bernice tried to be inconspicuous. "Let's walk a little ways. Ken will find us."

As they walked along, Ozzie switched from heeling on Bernice's left side, to walking on her right. "What are you doing?" His answer was a quiet growl. Ozzie never growled without a good reason. Bernice noticed a man standing in the doorway they passed. Ozzie walked faster.

"Let's stop here and wait for Ken," Bernice said. Ozzie stayed on her right side and looked back over his shoulder as Bernice stood at the curb. As Ken got closer, the man ran toward Bernice.

"Give me the bag, you old bat!" As he lunged for her purse, she sidestepped neatly off the curb. Her timing was perfect. Ken pulled up and Bernice and Ozzie got into the car.

As they drove off, Ken looked in the rearview

mirror. "Whatever is that man doing? Is that hip hop? He's some kind of street performer?"

Bernice looked in the side mirror. The parking meters here were much shorter than most. It would be easy for someone to run right into one with painful results. "I think that's what they call twerking."

*

"Look at him. A slider and a dessert waffle on top of that," Bernice said to Ozzie. Ken snoozed away in the recliner. "Let's go sort some beads."

Ozzie and Bernice went to her craft room on the second floor. "I'm going to give some of the beads I'll never use to the thrift store so I'll have room for the new ones. Ken won't be able to complain then. Look at these ugly yellow and green ones. Ethel said her granddaughter blew them out of glass. It looks like they're made of old Play-Doh. And pony beads. I don't need those." Bernice found she was talking to herself as Ozzie had dozed off too. "I guess your pulled pork waffle filled you up."

"Where is that receipt? I know I signed it. How can I check things off, if it's not here," Bernice muttered to herself as she pawed through the small bags. "Nothing. Well, okay then. I can just call the bank and ask them how much I spent."

The call to the bank was frustrating to say the least. There was a record of Ozzie's grooming charge and one for lunch at the waffle place. Nothing about a bead store. There was no name on the bag and Bernice didn't remember seeing a sign out front.

"Well, I can't be losing my mind totally. I mean, here are the beads. That's proof I was there. It must just be a computer snafu." Bernice was determined not to think about the effects of aging on the brain.

The pink piggies went into one compartment, the dogs in another. Cats, fish, frogs and birds followed. Bernice was having a fine afternoon.

Until she found the crystals.

"I know I didn't buy crystals today. I stuck with lampwork beads. Where have all these come from?" Bernice remembered that Paul had included a special treat for her, but this was too much. There were bags and bags, pink, pale blue, dark blue, red, green, yellow and clear stones. In the sunlight, they looked like bits of a stained glass window. Bernice reached for a magnifying glass.

"Ozzie, wake up!" The little dog was on his feet immediately. As Bernice turned, she brushed a pink pig off the table. "Get that pink piggy for me, will you? Thank you, that's a good boy. I'm going to put these crystals in a special place and we're going back to visit Paul to find out just what's going on."

Bernice went to the old thermostat on the wall. They'd installed a new digital one that Ken could work, and Bernice found puzzling. The old thermostat now had a new purpose. Pushing a button on its side, Bernice watched as the casing popped open.

Inside she gave a push on the wall and a small door swung out. "This is where they'll stay for now." She popped the door closed, and the casing back over it. "Let's go see if Ken's awake and ready for a walk." Ozzie beat her down the stairs.

*

"Go past the lava lamp place and then the furniture store, it's on the opposite side of the street from that." A couple of days had passed before Bernice could get Ken to go back to Cherokee Street. She had to promise he could stop at the hardware store for more nails and maybe they'd get another waffle.

"I'm not seeing it. Are you sure?"

"Just pull over and park here. I'll ask that man."

Bernice approached the window washer and watched his swirling squeegee for a minute. "Excuse me, can you tell me how to get to the bead shop? I could have sworn it was right here."

"The landlord told me this place has been vacant for a while. I don't know about any bead shop."

Ozzie tugged at his leash, eager to go into the empty store. "Do you mind if I take a look? I know of someone who wants to open a small shop." She made that part up, but Bernice felt it was for a good cause —her sanity.

"Will the dog behave? I don't want any, you know, mess in there."

"Oh sure. He's trained to go everywhere with me." That last part was a bit of a stretch.

"Okay, just until I finish this last window. Then I gotta lock up."

Bernice and Ozzie went inside. There was nothing left to remind her of the bead shop. "Ozzie, am I losing my mind? I swear this is where I was. Look, I can see the Wash and Woof from here. I *know* this is the place."

The window washer's moving shadow made the shop spooky in the afternoon light. Ozzie started to paw at the floor. "What are you doing? Come away from there." Ozzie refused. "Well, I'll be damned." In-between the old floorboards were a couple of stray beads. Bernice fished them out with a pin from her purse and put them in her pocket.

Pounding on the window startled her so much, she almost lost her balance. "Geez. lady, I'm sorry. I thought you heard me say I'm done. I didn't mean to scare you."

"I was just thinking about something else," Bernice said. "We're ready to go too."

The window washer locked the door and headed to his truck as Bernice and Ozzie walked to the car. "It's waffle time." She didn't look back.

*

Bernice checked, but no black car was in sight. She reassured herself that it was just her imagination. She'd always been a bit fanciful, and this was nothing new, really. The ride home was uneventful so she decided to reward herself with a little bead time.

"Darn it, Ozzie, I should have taken that bag of beads for the thrift shop. We could've dropped it off on the way," she said as they climbed the stairs. "I'll put it by the door next time."

When Bernice stepped into her craft room, she looked at the table where she'd left the bag, but the table was bare. "What the hell? Ozzie, I left it right here, I swear." Bernice was beginning to doubt her sanity, and her odds of needing a keeper, the way things were going.

As she stepped forward, she almost fell. Only grabbing the edge of the table kept her on her feet. Ozzie obligingly gave her the reason for her close call—one of the ugly green and yellow beads. "Somebody's..." She stopped herself before Ken heard.

"What's that? Did you slip? Really, Bernice, you've got to carry that cane."

"Just stepped on a bead," Bernice said. "How about I teach Ozzie to fetch my cane for me? If I drop it, he'd be a big help."

"Sounds like a good idea. You do that while I have a nap."

Bernice and Ozzie worked on "Cane" and "Bring It" off and on for an hour. Ozzie had the knack for picking up the cane, but it was apparent he needed to grab it in the middle. After he cleared the coffee table a couple of times, knocked over one lamp and had a near miss with the television, Bernice worked on his control. He looked like a little furry Walenda as he carefully walked across the floor without hitting anything.

Ozzie created a trick of his own, too. He liked to run between her legs while she stood at the table. Bernice had always heard, if there's an undesirable behavior, put it on cue. The dog will do it on command then and not as a surprise. Bernice called Ozzie's new trick Tween. By the end of Ken's nap, Ozzie had both tricks down pat.

"That calls for a treat! Let's go outside and sit in the sun with our afternoon tea," said Bernice. Tea was really wine and crackers for her and homemade dog cookies for Ozzie, but afternoon tea sounded, well, elegant, or at least more elegant than boxed wine. Elegant reminded her of Paul, so she gave the matter a lot of thought as she sipped.

*

Thursday was Bernice's day at the hospital as a Pink Lady. She fetched books and magazines and wrote letters for patients. Mostly, she listened as they talked, since many of them never had visitors.

"Bernice, you have a new patient in Room 402. He's just come down from Intensive Care. He's confused but that should clear up," said the Head Nurse. "If he asks, he was mugged. They found him down near the river, all banged up. Try to find out about him if you can. He had no I.D."

"I'll take these books to Mrs. Sullivan and then visit him."

Bernice had a nice chat with the old lady, well, really not that much older than Bernice herself, but either she seemed a lot older or Bernice felt a lot younger. It was time to visit 402's mystery guest.

"Hi, my name is Bernice. I'm a Pink Lady and I'm here to make your stay a little nicer. Would you like..." She'd backed into the room, pulling the book cart along, but when she turned, she dropped the book she'd chosen. "Good Lord, Paul, is that you? What the hell happened?"

Gone was the elegant, dashing man. Instead, a victim lay on the bed, sheet barely moving as he breathed. He motioned with his hand that she should shut the door.

He tried to smile but Bernice could see it hurt. How could it not? His lips were swollen and split. "Bernice..." It was just a whisper, but she was glad to know he'd remembered. "The crystals?"

"They're in a safe place where no one will find them. You were mugged. That's the official version. To me, it looks like a beating. Near the river so they could throw you in?" At his nod, she went on. "Nurse wants me to find out who you are and who we should call. Tell me only what I need to know. We'll sort the rest out later."

It took a while, but Bernice left the room with a phone number and a name. When the Head Nurse stopped her, Bernice said, "Sorry, couldn't make sense of anything he said except he was thirsty. I'll try again on Saturday." She took her break where she'd be sure of both privacy and cell phone reception.

*

On Fridays, Ken went to the Lodge for a meeting. Bernice knew it was an excuse to barbeque and drink beer, but since he always brought food home, she never complained. In any relationship, time apart was a good thing.

She spent part of the morning in the garden, weeding. She found she had pulled up some of the plants as well and had to put them back. "Ozzie, my mind is elsewhere. Let's have some lunch and talk out this bead thing. There's got to be something we can do. Waiting is a pain in the patoot." Ozzie agreed, but whether it was about lunch or the patoot, it was hard to say.

Bernice stepped into the kitchen and felt a hard push between her shoulder blades. As she fell, her cane skittered across the floor. She made sure she didn't land on her hands and break a wrist, but her shoulder hurt like hell. Thank goodness there were no snapping noises, like a hip giving way.

Ozzie growled and looked toward the door. It wasn't his low growl but a full-fledged, I'm-a-killer-dog version. Standing there was the would-be purse snatcher. "Hey there, old lady, guess what? I'm back," he said. "Damn, I hope that hurt you as much as the parking meter hurt me."

Bernice scooted around, facing more toward the

living room than the back door. "Somehow, I don't think it does. What do you want? We don't keep cash here and the television's too big to carry."

"Yeah, I found out about the cash part when I was here the other day," he said. "That's not what I'm looking for and you know it. Where are the jewels?" He paced around the kitchen, opened drawers and looked in the fridge.

"I'm not a jewels type. My ring is a gold band. Earrings make my ears itch. I'm afraid you've come to the wrong place." Ozzie looked like he was ready to attack. Bernice gave him the Calm Puppy signal.

"Don't act the fool. I want the jewels you got from the old man. They're going to fund my retirement to a nice warm climate." He circled around in front of her. "What a crock, to think a couple of geezers could fool me. The old guy had to hand them off and you were the only customer. The company must be hard up for couriers if they've resorted to the Medicare crowd. You'd be better off as a Walmart greeter."

Although Ozzie's instinct was to get between the man and Bernice, she'd given him a hand signal to back up. He followed the command without question.

The man stood, feet apart, a yard or so away from Bernice, and spread his arms wide. "So what's it going to be, dingbat? You gonna hand over the jewels now or after I break a few fingers?"

"You know, I really don't like your tone," Bernice said. "Ozzie, Cane! Tween—go fast!"

Ozzie grabbed the cane in the middle as they'd trained and ran to Bernice, right between the man's legs. Each end of the cane hit him squarely behind his knees. Bernice loved the way he looked as he fell—arms windmilling, legs flying, and then the satisfying crack as his head hit the tile floor.

"Ozzie, call 9-1-1. It's going to take me a minute to get up."

*

"Ma'am, you'll have to wear this sling for a few days to let your shoulder muscles heal. It's a wonder you weren't hurt worse. Good thing you have the One Big Button phone your dog can dial." The paramedic had no idea.

Ken had come home just as the police and ambulance arrived. Ken was so panicked Bernice worried he'd need the ambulance more than she did.

"God, Bernice, you scared the crap out of me! What can I do, honey? You need a drink? I do. Oh, I forgot the barbeque in the car."

"Ken, slow down. The food won't spoil in the next two minutes. If you want something to do, make a phone call for me. Just tell the man who answers what you found when you got home today. Tell him everything's okay. I'll explain it later."

"You're sure?"

"Yes, just make the call."

*

Bernice didn't go to the hospital. She'd be there

the next day for Pink Lady duty anyway. For now, she wanted a little piece and quiet.

On Saturday, the Head Nurse told her that her patient in Room 402 had been transferred. "Some relative showed up and I.D.'d him. They took him to a private hospital. He'll get more rest there. If you're sure you want to work your shift, I have a Candy Striper who can help with the book cart."

*

Sunday, Bernice was surprised to hear a knock at the front door. Ozzie didn't growl so that was a plus. "Do you know who I am?" The man wore a black suit, and a shirt white enough to star in its own commercial. The sunglasses were a nice touch.

"Not by name, but I recognize your voice. You answered the phone when I called about my friend. Will you come in?"

"No thank you. I'm here on his behalf. You helped him so he'd like to fulfill your wish," he said. He lifted his wrist and said, "Bring the truck."

Bernice heard the beep-beep-beep of a backing truck that took up the whole driveway. Four guys jumped out and opened the overhead door. "The men will help you arrange everything. Want a look?"

Bernice and Ozzie stood behind the truck, mouths open. The inside of the truck fairly glowed as Bernice remembered saying, "If it was up to me, I'd own every bead in this store."

From Hay to Eternity

"Welcome to the hayride. Listen up! Find a seat on the bench or one of the hay bales and hold on. Our horse, Sam, sometimes rocks the wagon when he starts, but it will be a smooth ride after that," said Darren Taylor. "Gus, our old scarecrow, is going to guide us around the farm. Sam knows the route, so even if Gus gets lost, we'll be able to find our way back. How about we let the families with little kids get on first?"

Everybody laughed when a red-headed boy wanted to know why Gus didn't just use a GPS.

One dad helped his kids onto the wagon and then the moms. A threat of no candy apples broke up a fight between two brothers. Pretty soon, everybody had a seat. The teenagers sat near the rear, young enough to want to go, but too cool to show they enjoyed it.

At the last minute, a scantily clad teenage girl was helped onto the wagon by Darren's brother, Todd.

"Hey, bro. Glad we caught you. Tiffany here loves a hayride, isn't that right, babe? I'll take some candid shots of her while we ride," Todd said. "Don't mind us, everybody. Tiffany's making her portfolio so she can be on *America's Next Top Model.*"

Darren pulled his brother aside. "What do you think you're doing? This is a ride for kids, not a way for you to promote your bimbo."

"Hey, Dad said it was okay. I stopped by earlier and asked, so back off." Todd was mere inches from Darren's face. "This is my home too, you know."

"No wonder Dad's not feeling up to going along tonight. You've been badgering him about selling again, haven't you?"

"Not at all." Todd smiled. "We had a very pleasant chat. Come on, Bree. Your sister needs somebody to hold the lights so I can take pictures.

A much younger girl, freckled, with a straight up and down figure, hopped onto the wagon. "She's got as much chance of being the next top model as that scarecrow does," said Bree. "She's seventeen, and in model years, that's ancient. Model years are worse than dog years." She ignored both Tiffany's pout and Todd's glare.

Tiffany wore what used to be called Daisy Dukes, tiny cut-off jean shorts and a top I'd heard referred to as a Rawhide—as in round 'em up, head 'em out, show what your mama gave you. Her cleavage rivaled the Grand Canyon. Dads and teenage boys took a sudden interest in the night sky.

"Sam, take us for a ride." Todd's arrival had dropped the Family Fun Factor to nearly zero.

The wagon lurched off and a few little girls squealed, more for the fun of it than from fear. The old scarecrow bobbed from side to side. A couple of times, he looked like he was going to fall off, but then would rock back the other way and keep on going. Darren talked about the history of the farm, back to the first Taylors to settle in the area and how the farm grew cucumbers, sweet corn, beans and vegetables of all kinds. Cantaloupe and watermelon were the highlight of the summer. A BLT wasn't complete without their heirloom tomatoes. Every fall, you could choose your own pumpkins for Halloween.

One of the little boys wanted to know why people just didn't go to the store, and a little girl asked if it was all organic. Darren was patient with all of them.

I go along on the tours because I'm qualified to give first aid if somebody gets a splinter or a bloody nose. It's a peaceful ride and I've done it so often, I could recite the history myself. Fred, Darren and Todd's dad, the owner of the farm, is a friend of mine. He and I go way back, to grade school. He loves the land like I love animals.

When Herbert, down the road, couldn't take care of Bessie, his old milk cow anymore, I talked Fred into taking her. Then came Myrt, the talkative pig. A couple of goats, a cranky old rooster and the horse followed. We had us a petting zoo of sorts.

Then one of the big box stores moved to town and started selling groceries. People got busy, and instead of coming to the farm to buy their produce, they stopped at the box store on the way home and bought carrots already cut up and shipped from a thousand miles away. For the love of Pete, who doesn't have time to peel a carrot?

Fred got older too. Arthritis slowed him down. Darren tried to help, but there was so much to do, and no one wanted to work the land anymore. Todd wanted to sell. Fred flat out told him, "Over my dead body." Todd said he was sure something like that could be worked out and mumbled about a competency hearing.

Todd's greatest ambition was to do nothing and have someone else take care of all his needs. Darren was just the opposite, a hard worker who would love nothing more than to live out his life on the farm, just like Bessie, Sam and the goats.

We came around the final turn and headed back. A full moon was just coming into view. Off in the distance, a wolf howled and got an answer. The air was crisp, a perfect fall evening, leaves ready to turn from soft green to bright gold, orange, yellow and red.

The only disruption was Todd's voice and his camera. Darren had to interrupt his talk several times. "No, Tiffany, you can't stand at the front of the wagon and pose like Rose from the *Titanic* movie." "No, Todd, she can't hold the reins." When he lost patience, it was "Dammit, Todd, NO! We can't stop the wagon so she can have her picture taken with the horse!"

That got him a dirty look from several of the mothers, but one was particularly upset when her three-year-old son started singing "Dammit, dammit, dammit, Todd." A discussion of who likes s'mores helped divert a mutiny.

Back at the house, dads helped moms and sleepy kids off the wagon. The littlest ones headed for the picnic tables where they'd get their s'mores and hot chocolate before heading home to bed. Darren lit a small fire for toasting the marshmallows.

The teenagers hung around to see Todd's photo shoot. Moms herded dads and kids into the store for cider and souvenirs, muttering "Don't you dare look." It wasn't clear if they meant the kids or the husbands.

Tiffany seemed to have one pose—legs straight, butt up and out, bent over at the waist and a toothy smile whiter than moonlight. "Tyra says that's a hoochie tooch pose! Don't show everything at once," Bree hollered to her sister. "Show some angulation with your legs. You might as well be standing on tree stumps."

I think Tiffany had a snappy comeback to give but it was going to take her a while to find it. In the meantime, she went back to simpering for the camera. "Smize, Tif, smize!" Bree shook her head.

"Tyra says that means smile with your eyes. Tif's never gonna be on that show."

"What's that on her, um, butt?" I said. "I think she sat on something."

"Naw, that's her tat," said Bree. Seeing my confusion, she said, "Tattoo. It's a Q, for SusieQ, her stage name. She says it's like, her signature." She raised her voice. "Why anybody is dumb enough to put their signature on their butt is beyond me."

"Todd, let's just do the scary Halloween thing we talked about." Tiffany stuck her tongue out at Bree. "We need to get that up on YouTube as soon as we can, so I can be virus by the 31st."

I looked to Bree for a translation. "She means *viral*, like when a video gets like a million hits. She says it's part of her platform." She shrugged. "Like she knows what that means."

Tiffany did a few poses near the scarecrow. One included its hand on her butt and a shocked look on her face. "I could get one of the goats to poke her with a cold nose," I said. "Then she'd have a real shocked look." Bree just grinned.

Finally, Todd handed Tiffany a big knife. Apparently it was time for the finale. "Okay, you remember what you're supposed to do? Scream a couple of times and then stab the scarecrow. Look scared and then real mad as you get your revenge," Todd gave the instructions. "Ready? Action!"

Tiffany gave her impersonation of a scared girl,

who I thought looked more constipated than afraid. She grabbed the knife from the seat of the wagon and slashed out. Blood erupted and covered her face and most of the rest of her skin, seeing as it was all exposed like.

"What the hell? This didn't happen when we rehearsed this afternoon!" It was about then she wiped her face and realized her hands were all red. "Oh. My. God." That was all she got out before she keeled over backwards, fell off the wagon and landed on her signature tat.

It's a good thing the picnic table for the little kids is around the side of the old house. They didn't see a thing. Deputy Sykes was on hand since his kids were among the group from the Scouts. He took charge right away.

When all was said and done, Sykes had to tell Darren and Todd that Gus the scarecrow was really Fred, their dad. The ambulance arrived within minutes, but it was still too late.

*

The funeral was held on the farm. Bessie, Mryt and Sam were in attendance, which Todd thought was disrespectful. They seemed more mournful than he did. I caught him taking pictures of the house and outbuildings and texting them to a realtor. Tiffany was a no-show, although Bree came by to help with Myrt.

Right after the service, Deputy Sykes took Todd

into custody. The autopsy showed Fred had a high level of his blood thinner and a sedative in him when he died. It explained why he didn't fight back or call out when Tiffany went at him with the knife, and why he bled so much, so fast.

It was Sykes's theory that Todd talked to Fred once again about selling the farm. Todd had lined up realtors and investors for a self-contained communal living space, which I think means rich people get in, everybody else stays out—unless you're the help. He said it would mean jobs and put the land to better use. When Fred said no, Todd drugged Fred's coffee, dressed him as Gus and propped him up on the wagon, using a rope to keep him in place during the ride.

His plan was for Tiffany to do the actual killing with what she thought was a prop knife on a prop scarecrow. Sykes said she wasn't smart enough to understand, even now, how she'd been set up. She was pretty pleased though that the video of the killing had gone "virus" so she could enjoy her fame. As Bree predicted, she never did get to be on *America's Next Top Model*, but her appearances on *Maury* and *Jerry Springer* got her quite the following. There's talk of a movie.

Darren got the farm and will live out his life here, just like the animals. He's dating Shelby, Bree's cousin. I think they have a future, so there will be Taylors on the land for a while longer.

Bree hangs out with me and Darren, feeding the animals. There are more now, so Darren got us non-profit status as a farm animal sanctuary. Myrt still entertains the kids with her oinking commentary. Sam pulls the wagon and is paid in all the apple slices he wants. At his age, he deserves them.

I'm doing all right. I miss Fred, but honestly, he didn't want to live all crippled up and unable to work. He died quickly and without pain.

Todd? He's still swearing his innocence to any-body who will listen, but that's not many people and none from around here. He got his wish too—some-body is taking care of all his needs, like a place to live and meals, and he can sit around and do nothing. Life in prison is like that.

Fred told me once, some people get what they want and some people get what they deserve. It's rare but once in a while, if you're lucky, what's wanted and what's deserved are the same thing.

I guess you could say everything worked out for the best.

Just like Fred and I planned it.

Todd should have known—if Fred said "Over my dead body," he'd mean it.

Deirdre and the Diamonds

"I dunno, Boss, the guy didn't hardly talk to no one," Rocko said. "We done like you tole us. Moose spilt a drink on his jacket and Marcus, the old dude who's the um, valet? in the men's, checked all his pockets and stuff. He dint have the jewels on him."

"Didn't hardly talk to no one? So he did talk to *someone.*"

"Well, there was this um, girl, kinda. She come into the place and run up to him and said, 'Uncle Albert, it's me,' and then kinda threw herself on him. I ain't never seen no girl kiss an uncle on the mouth like that before." Rocko was in awe. "He got all red in the face and pushed her away. The main waiter guy, he come over and told her to leave. She kinda flounced outta there."

"This girl, what did she look like?"

"Well, she was wearing a school uniform, like from one of them Catholic schools. A white blouse, short skirt, kinda rolled up around the middle." Rocko looked at Moose. "Right?"

"Yeah, her belly button showed. Ma won't let my sister go out lookin' like that." Moose chimed in.

"She had on these dark stockings, the kind that stay up by theirself, and her hair was in pigtails. She was carrying some kind of big purse too."

"Shoes," Moose said.

"Oh yeah, them Mary Jane strappy kind with heels. My cousin has a pair of 'em. But she's a hooker," said Rocko. "Oh hey Boss, do you think this girl was like a hooker too? She looked real nice."

"No, you idiots, I think this girl was like a courier and she picked up the package right in front of you! If you hadn't been so focused on shoes and stockings, you'd have seen it," the Boss said. "Get out of my sight and hope I don't decide to make an example out of the two of you. Thanks to you, we missed out on an opportunity to steal a whole lot of diamonds."

The two men slunk out of the office and down the hall. "Geez, the Boss was pretty mad. Do you think he's gonna like kill us?"

"Nah, he'll get over it, but I bet he calls Ma and tells her we screwed up again."

"Geez, she'll never let it go. Maybe we oughta go to the casino until she calms down," Moose said. "It's all-you-can-eat seafood night."

"What do you bet Ma's at the casino? Hey, she'll be at the slots and we'll be eating. It'll be okay."

*

After Deidre pulled the bag of diamonds from

the back of the courier's collar, she stuffed it, well, no one needs the details of just where it went next. She trotted around the back of the restaurant, looked back to see if anyone followed and slipped into the kitchen where Jorge waited.

"The coast is clear, chica, but hurry, it's almost time for the lunch rush."

"I won't be long, I promise." She slipped him a fifty and headed for the storeroom. Once there, the cheap blouse came off and she stepped out of the short skirt. A longer, tweedy skirt hid any sexiness of the stockings and turned them into old-lady support hose. A plain white blouse buttoned to the neck ("Damn."), wrinkled again, with a jacket was next. Pigtails down, bun up, makeup taken off with a wipe. The wipe put into a baggie and into the purse that, turned inside out, now resembled a soft briefcase. Dangly earrings off, button pearls on, glasses too, what else? Shoes—off with the Mary Janes and on with sensible pumps.

The transformation from hot to frump was complete. Deidre grabbed a clipboard and pen and exited the storeroom. "Chica, you look awful and it only took four minutes," said Jorge. "A new record."

"I practice, Jorge. Now for the health inspector to give you a glowing review," she said. "I'll see you soon. Buy something nice for the kids with that money."

"You got it."

She made an obvious entrance into the dining

room, clipboard in hand, approached random tables to ask if the food had been hot enough when served and spot checked silverware for cleanliness, mentioning that Jorge's kitchen always got the highest scores of any restaurant. It never hurt to put in a good word here and there.

Two minutes later, she was in a cab and headed back to the office, another cab close behind.

*

Deidre paid the cabbie and headed for her building, absent-mindedly patting her left pocket. As she crossed the alley, a homeless man pushed his shopping cart into her path. She grabbed at it to keep from falling but still banged her leg and dropped her purse, spilling a few items. A false bottom kept the hottie outfit tucked out of sight.

Hands pulled her back as Krueger, obvious as all get out, but in the guise of a Good Samaritan, set Deidre on her feet. In what he considered a subtle move, he dipped his left hand into her pocket, which, thank goodness, was at waist level. "You nearly ran this lady over. I should call a cop," he said to the homeless man. Like that would ever happen.

"Damn it, you better not have torn my stockings." She turned an ankle left and right. "You lucked out this time. Watch where you're going." Krueger handed her the spillage. She stuffed everything back into the bag, hitched it firmly on her shoulder and sighed as the homeless guy fought to turn his cart to the right and headed off without a word of apology.

"Are you all right, Miss?"

"Yes, I'm fine. Thank you for coming to my rescue." That laid it on a little thick but Krueger ate that kind of thing right up.

"Anything to help." *Subtle* and *Krueger* would never be in the same thought. "You might want to get that jacket cleaned. Who knows what kind of germs are on there now?"

Any germs were more likely to be from his hands—who knew where they'd been—than the shopping cart, but she said, "I will. It's so hard to find someone with good manners these days. Everyone's in too much of a rush to stop and help."

"Well, I like to think my little old mother would be proud of me," he said. "If you're sure you're all right, I'll be on my way."

"I'm sure, thanks."

Deidre watched as he wandered down the street. Inside the building, she waited to make sure he didn't double back before she got on the elevator. After the doors closed, she used a key that allowed her to access the top floor, not listed on the main panel.

The hallway showed offices, some with the door hanging open, some with names half scraped off. There was no sign of life, no sound, and the dingy carpet muffled her own steps. She entered the third door to the left, went past the receptionist's vacant desk and through the closet.

"Took you long enough. You saw Krueger? Jake timed it just right?"

"Who could miss Krueger? He's such an obvious tail. He said his little old mother would be proud of his manners for helping me. He's the worst pickpocket ever. My granny could do a better lift."

"Deidre, your granny wrote the book on how to get the goods. I sat behind her in church last week. She put a single in the collection plate and took out two twenties. I watched and still couldn't catch her," Mavis said. "Krueger can tell his little old mommy about it when he visits her. She's pulling seven to twelve in the state pen."

"So you went to church to learn how to steal?" Deidre laughed as she took off the frumpy jacket and let down her hair. "Mavis, you're lucky God let you in."

"I did not! I had a new hat. That's a perfectly good reason to go to church." Mavis pulled out her cell phone. "Look, here's a picture of it. I figure with a hat like that, no one will remember what *I* look like, just the hat." The hat was bright yellow with dips and swirls, feathers, dangles, ribbon and a few other things Deidre couldn't make out. One might have been a squirrel, but it was best not to know for sure.

"That's some hat. Jake's timing with the shopping cart was perfect. I slipped the diamonds in it before

Krueger got within three feet of me. Jake should be at the post office, mailing them to the client and getting thrown out about now. Thank goodness for prepaid packages so he doesn't have to get in line. They hate that cart of his. The wobbly wheel was a great touch."

"I don't know why you took that job. You know they haven't paid their invoices for the last three months," Mavis said. She liked a balanced set of books.

"Looky here, what's this?" Deidre hiked up the frump skirt and fumbled with the top of her stocking. "Do you think these will cover their tab?" She laid two full-carat, pear-shaped diamonds on the desk.

"Oh my, I think so." Mavis held the diamonds up to her ears. "They'd make a fabulous Christmas bonus for a devoted employee."

"Would Jake wear something that splashy?"

"Smart ass. I'll put them in the safe before I'm tempted." Mavis pushed a printout of phone calls toward Deidre. "Here's the cream of the crop. The rest were cranks. Coffee's fresh."

Deidre poured a cup. "Why's Andrew calling again? He didn't believe us the last six times we told him his wife was cheating on him? That woman could do a jackass in Times Square and he'd still take her back."

"Remember the pictures of her with that goon? She *was* doing a jackass, just not in Times Square.

Andrew says he loves her, poor guy. I swear she knows we're following and poses for those shots. It's too easy otherwise."

Deidre and Mavis went over the call list. "Tell these clowns no. Too dangerous for too little and I don't work for people I don't like. These guys yes, find out when they need answers. These I'll think about, tell them they'll know in a few days."

She walked toward her office. "Send this suit to the cleaners. Krueger touched it. I'm itchy already. We'll talk about the diamonds later."

*

The next morning, it was time for the weekly meeting. Jake was late, not a rare thing, but rare enough to cause comment. "Straight to voice mail," said Mavis. "Maybe he's hung over. Or..."

"Or was beamed up to the mother ship?" Deidre was a bit worried. "Let's get on with the meeting. First up, whose turn is it to do the photo shoot of Andrew's wife?"

Assignments were made and operatives headed out. Still no Jake. A glance at Mavis rated a head shake.

"We just wait?"

"Let's give him until lunch and then we'll go to Plan B," Deidre said. "Surely we'll hear by then."

"I'll make a list of places to look," said Mavis. "It'll give me something to do besides worry." She turned on the television.

At 10:30, a special report interrupted regularly scheduled programming. "Police Chief John Adams announced that at 9:37 this morning, a black car of foreign make slowed as it passed the main police station. The rear door opened and the body of a man, badly beaten, was thrown from the vehicle. Witnesses were unable to give a description of other passengers or the driver because of dark tinted windows. Chief Adams said it appears every bone in the man's hands were broken. We'll have more information as it's available. Now for a word from our sponsors, Twinky-Dink Confectionary."

Mavis had to put her head on her knees. Deidre would have liked to be more sympathetic but she was having trouble breathing herself. "It's not Jake. You'll see," she said. Mavis nodded, sat up, took a deep breath and continued with her list.

During the 11:30 news update, the announcer reported, "Another man has been treated at a local hospital. Similar to the attack we reported earlier, every bone in his hand had been broken, although in this case, only the left hand, not both. Due to privacy issues, no further details were available. Police had no comment. There is speculation this is part of a gang initiation or perhaps punishment for someone who stole drugs from the gangs. In happier news, this week's Pet of the Week is Chipper, a blue parakeet who belongs to Alice Simpkins. She and Chipper have won a $25 gift certificate to Seed 'N Feed so

Chipper can pick out his own treats." Mavis smacked the Off button so hard, Deidre thought she might have broken the remote entirely.

"The only people speculating about drugs and gangs are reporters," Deidre said. "I'd bet they're talking about Krueger. He's left-handed. Breaking the bones would be a good way to get him to tell about following me."

"Who's your guess for the dead guy then?" Mavis refused to make eye contact.

"The courier. He lost the diamonds so that would make them cranky. Have Tony's guys narrowed down Jake's location? Thank goodness for traffic and security cameras and guys who can hack into them."

"Yes, they're down to three warehouses, on the docks, easier to get in and out with weapons, and lots of hiding places to choose from. When the phone call comes, we'll know."

Lunchtime came and went, although neither of them had any appetite. When the phone rang just after one o'clock, Mavis leapt at it. "Exterminations and Eradications, how may I direct your call?" She and Diedre were head to head, both listening.

"You have something of mine. I want it back." The voice was smooth, no trace of an accent. "Let me talk to the girl, the one who took my merchandise." Mavis passed the phone to Deidre.

"I have many things other people want. What's on your mind?"

"I want the diamonds."

"How unfortunate."

"They were presold. You've caused me...difficulties."

"So sorry but you've caused *me* difficulties as well. I don't like being inconvenienced. You have my man. What do you suggest?"

"A trade."

"Put him on the phone."

In the background, she heard a voice say, "Tell her where you are, and there'll be a bullet in your knee."

"Sorry I missed the meeting," Jake's voice slurred, more likely from a fat lip than from too much Scotch. "Do me a favor, record my shows? The Brando one, *Jump Street* and Mac. I'm not sure what time I'll be done here."

"Sure, why not? You want me to pick up pizza too? You know I'm going to have to dock you for the time off."

"Atta girl, four or five slices would do the trick," Jake said. His voice faded but she heard a faint "Ow!" before the smooth-voiced man came on the line.

"This is just like in a store—you break it, you buy it," Deidre said. "A few dings and dents are acceptable, but any real damage will be a problem...for you."

"He's fine, just tripped over his own feet. If you

want him back, bring me the diamonds. We'll meet behind the library at midnight."

"Well, *want* him back, might be a little strong. On the other hand, it would be easier than training someone new. However, it's not an even swap. I want money *and* my man."

"You are in no position to bargain."

"Oh, but I think I am. You need the diamonds more than I need him. After all, how good can he be if he let himself get caught by the likes of you? By the way, love your accent, South African, am I right?"

"I *have* no accent! Be at the library tonight. You'll get your money and this low life who works for you. If not, his body will be on your doorstep in the morning." The phone slammed down in her ear.

"Well, they're going old school. You can't slam a cell phone like that. See if it can be traced. Did you follow the clues Jake gave us?"

Mavis nodded, "Brando is *On the Waterfront, Jump Street* means Pier 21 and Mac is MacGyver so we get to blow something up! Four or five slices, bring Tony and his guys. You said dock him so he knows you understood. Should I make the calls?"

"Yes, let's go at eight o'clock. It will be dark but early enough they won't expect us. Get word to Alf that we'll leave a package all tied up nice and pretty for him. He can be on the ten o'clock news." Mavis grinned and made another list—C4, det cord, duct tape...

*

Deidre, Mavis and several operatives met Tony on Pier 21. "What's the status?"

"Infrared says we got one person laying down, three on their feet. My guys have spotted two patrolling outside. They'll take care of them on your say so. We got a complication though, a guy we found wandering around the area," Tony said. "He says he kinda knows you." Tony motioned into the darkness. One of his men dragged the intruder into the light.

"Krueger, nice to see you again. How'd you find us?" Deidre wasn't happy with the interruption.

"I was motivated." Krueger held up his left hand, huge with a plaster cast and supported in a sling. "I was supposed to get the package from the old guy and deliver it. You intercepted. They weren't happy."

"Who's they?"

"Look, I'll tell you, and I'd like a favor. Right, I know I'm not in a position to ask, but I'm invested, okay?" At her nod, he continued, "The guys took care of the courier and dumped him at the police station. They're not too bright. That kind of thing works better when they're on their home turf. Anyway, then they started on me. I told them where I saw you last. They don't know which building you went in."

"It would be easier to chuck you off the pier. With that hand, you'd sink like a big old rock."

"Even with both hands working, I'm not much of

a swimmer. Here's what I know. The package is full of blood diamonds. You know what those are?"

"Yeah, stolen, sold to raise money for a revolution or war of some kind. They call them conflict diamonds too. Just what South Africa doesn't need right now." Deidre paced as she thought.

"These guys are clueless. This is a one-shot. They want to make a trade?" Krueger said. "You know they don't intend to keep their part of the deal, or you wouldn't be here. What if I come in at the end? I'd like a little payback."

"Tony, if he makes a sound louder than a breath, chuck him into the water. Show Mavis the infrared. She needs to know where to put the det cord."

Mavis could move more quietly than most mice. She had the det cord attached to the side wall in no time. "Don't forget, I didn't take it to ground level. The last time I did that, we broke a water main and liked to drown ourselves before we made the recovery. The hole will be six inches up so step over. Don't go falling face first through my newly made door."

"Got it. No drowning, no falling. The C4 planted?"

"Yep. Nothing too big, but splashy and impressive. It'll get their attention."

Deidre pressed her ear bud. "Ready to go?" The men responded. "On my count, five, four, three, two..." She pointed to Mavis who pressed a button. Several explosions erupted on the west side of the building. Tony reported the guards were running in that direction. Mavis pressed more buttons and fire leapt into the sky on the north side.

"One guy, still laying down, guess that's Jake," said Tony. "One watching him, the others headed for the fire."

Mavis smiled and pressed the last button. The whoomp shook the dock, but no hole appeared in the wall. "What the hell? I put enough det cord on that thing to open Fort Knox." She ran for the building, Deidre close behind.

"Watch yourselves, the blast musta knocked down the drywall," Tony said into the ear buds. "The inside guard's on the other side of the wall from you."

Mavis shook her head. The det cord should have opened a hole big enough for a marching band. She put a hand on the wall and gave a little push. Much to her surprise, the wall gave way and fell inward. *deleted "steel"

"Cool move, the guard is down, I'm guessing under the wall," said Tony. "Get in and get out. My guys are rounding up the others now."

"As soon as we recover Jake, bring Krueger."

Mavis stepped through the opening and ignored the moans of the man beneath the broken wall as she walked across it. Deidre followed. Jake sat up, brushed drywall crumbs out of his hair and shook his head. "Geez, what took you girls so long?"

"Get your butt up and out of here. Do you know Mavis had to use the last of her det cord to blow this joint? She'll be docking your paycheck." Deidre helped Jake to his feet and they limped out through Mavis's door, still ignoring the screaming man beneath it. Two of Tony's men went in to fetch him.

Outside, Krueger identified the captured men. "That one's the ring leader, Gustav Pierson. He did all the bossing. The rest just followed orders," said Krueger. "Pierson's the one who told them to break my hand."

Tony snapped his fingers and two of his men brought forward large cobblestones from the end of the pier. "You wanna do the honors?" he asked Krueger. "The boys will give you a hand, pardon the pun."

"Sure, appreciate the help." Krueger stepped closer to Pierson. Three of Tony's men held Pierson flat on the pier while another passed a cobblestone to Krueger and helped him steady it. Without warning, Krueger dropped the stone on Pierson's outstretched left hand. "One is enough for me, although I think he deserves the other for the courier."

"Done," said Tony. And it was.

*

In front of Deidre's building, Krueger took his leave. "I'm heading home. I'll have to call Moms up at State before she gets all worried, tell her I'm okay. Thanks, really."

"What are you going to do now?" Deidre nodded

at his bandaged hand. "Your line of work won't allow for that."

"Hey, I never was a good pickpocket, you know that. It was Moms, she wanted me to carry on the family business. Now I got an excuse to start over. I'm gonna go straight, kinda. My brother-in-law's got an insurance agency. Ain't that a hoot? Layin' a bet that something's gonna happen and losing your money if it doesn't. And they call that legit?" Krueger turned to go. "If there's ever anything I can do for you, all you gotta do is say. Really." He waved his good hand and flagged down a cab.

*

The late news was on the big screen television. The newscaster got a serious look on his face and announced, "In breaking news, Interpol, in conjunction with the FBI, has captured five South African men, presumed to be terrorists. Four of the men were intent on funding an uprising against their government, while their leader, career criminal Gustav Pierson, seemed to have his own agenda. Let's go live to Brock Andersen, KTFU's own investigative reporter, on the scene at Pier 21. Are you there, Brock?"

"Yes, Brock Andersen, KTFU's investigative reporter here, live on the scene at Pier 21." The reporter's voice came through first, then the picture, just as Brock reached up to smooth down his comb-over. "It's a gruesome scene so those viewers who are squeamish should avert their eyes for this next part.

Gustav Pierson, ring leader of the terrorists, is being loaded into an ambulance here on Pier 21. Paramedics report they had to move two heavy cobblestones," Brock said. He pointed to the big blocks of stone and noted the blood on them. "The stones were smashed down on his hands, breaking every bone. One has to wonder, does this have anything to do with similar incidents earlier today? To answer those questions and more, here's Interpol Agent, Alf Davis." Terrorists, hot damn, Brock could smell an Emmy.

"Due to increased chatter, we were able to ascertain terrorists would illegally enter the country this week. Our agents, in cooperation with the FBI and local authorities, intercepted phone calls between Pierson and an unknown party where he seemingly solicited funds. Pierson planned to build bombs in this abandoned warehouse, which allows for an easy water escape," Davis said as the cameras panned the area. "So far, we do not have information on where the bombs would have been placed. As luck would have it, they are not very good bomb makers. The bombs detonated while being assembled and resulted in the chaos viewers see behind us. However, rest assured, thanks to the dedicated agents of Interpol and the FBI, the city remains safe." Alf maintained his solemn demeanor. The corner of a piece of paper could be seen sticking out of Alf's pocket. Deidre, Mavis and Jake threw popcorn at the television screen.

"They didn't even mention the diamonds." Deidre

threw more popcorn. "Next time, old Alf can wear the hottie outfit."

"He doesn't have the legs for it." Jake added his two cents and a few pieces of popcorn.

"*They* made the bombs?" Mavis contributed a handful to the airborne flurry.

"And when did I get to be an unknown party?" Deidre was on a roll. "Soliciting funds from me? Good grief."

"I just wish people could see what it says on the note in his pocket. That would raise a few eyebrows." Jake had written the note himself and pinned it to Pierson's jacket.

> *I am Gustav Pierson, a terrorist. My men and I have smuggled blood diamonds into your country to cause chaos and bring harm to your people while funding a revolution in our own country. My men wish to serve their sentences in your prisons, but I request to be extradited back to South Africa as a political statement. I waive my right to an attorney or assistance from the South African embassy.*

"That ought to fix Pierson right up. Especially since he can't talk, write or walk."

"Talk or walk? What happened that I missed?" Deidre said.

"I think Pierson tried to trip one of Tony's boys who shot Pierson in the kneecap. One of the others might have stepped on his larynx, just to keep the moaning and groaning to a minimum. He was using bad language too. You know how Mavis feels about that."

"Damn right," said Mavis. "God made enough words for us to use. No call to start cussing."

"Let me explain to old Brock here, *I* found out about these clowns, *I* figured out about the diamonds, *I* lifted them." Deidre saved some popcorn for herself.

"And *I*, the good-looking one, mailed them to Alf," said Jake.

"*I*, the smart one, found a briefcase in the warehouse and brought it with me," said Mavis. She pulled it from under a cushion. The case was full of cash. "I already took enough for our expenses and gave us each a nice bonus, Tony and the boys too. What should we do with the rest?"

"It should go to the guy who told me about the diamonds in the first place. He'll be able to put it to good use," said Deidre. "Agreed?" They were.

*

Deidre entered the small storefront office. "Ah, my friend, I am so glad you are looking well. I saw the news and worried your health might have suffered because of my selfish request," said the man behind the counter. His smile lit the room. "Might I offer you refreshment?"

"I'd love a cup of that sweet coffee we had last time."

After they'd settled at a small table, Deidre said, "And you? Are the boys adjusting?"

"We have ongoing medical issues, of course. They suffered so before leaving our homeland. So many war orphans. To be homeless and beg for food on the streets is bad enough. To be taken and forced to work in the diamond mines, is dangerous. Many of the boys are crippled or missing limbs due to cave-ins or blasting. However, we must have hope. These boys are here where they can get medical help. They are all doing well in school, even Iru, who now reads English at first-grade level, thanks to your suggestion he read to the dog."

"I'm glad. Every boy should have a dog."

"We have more boys arriving next week. I do not know where we will put them, but God will provide." The man smiled in spite of the worry lines on his forehead.

"I've heard there's a warehouse on the pier that was recently sold for a mere pittance due to damage it sustained. I believe it would make a wonderful home for the boys. You must go and see. Make any suggestions you like for the interior. Tony is the man to talk to. He'll take care of everything," Deidre said. "The coffee was wonderful, as always."

As she rose to leave, the man said, "But wait,

you've forgotten your briefcase." He started to pass it to her.

"Keep it and use it well."

Deidre paused at the door. She heard just what she expected.

"Boys, boys, come quick! Oh my, oh my, God surely did provide!"

Bananas Foster

"That little twit! Who does he think he is?" Bernice yelled as she stomped around the bedroom. "He looks like he's twelve years old and he's going to tell me *I'm* crazy? I should've just smacked him!"

"He didn't say you were crazy. He said you're getting older. He probably talks like that to all the old people." Ken edged toward the door. Saying "old" had been a mistake.

Bernice came at him like a heat-seeking missile, arms pin wheeling and one finger pointing. At least it was the index finger. Judging by the color of her face, her blood pressure medicine was failing to keep pace with her rant. "*Old?* I can still get pantyhose on without any help. I don't wear raggedy old granny panties. And colored bras—who do you know who has more colored bras than I do, I'd like to know? *Old* women wear white underwear." Bernice went on. "I work at the hospital as a Pink Lady. Do you think they let crazy people do that? *They* don't think I'm old!"

Ken saw a way out of the conversation. "Bernice,

it's almost time for your shift. Shouldn't you be getting all pinked up?"

*

"Okay, all you people out of the room. John is acting like a big crab ass and needs some Pink Time. Come back in an hour or so. He'll either be in a better mood or I'll have used the Big Pillow and put him out of my misery," Bernice said as she shooed them to the door. The relatives all filed out of the hospital room in slow motion. "Out, out, out. Go sit in the garden and smell the flowers or something."

John said, "You sure are bossy today, Bernice. What's got you in a mood?"

"Ah the doctor talked to me like I was a geezer. Little snot. Said I should take up a project, try something new or do something I used to enjoy. I think he meant knitting or quilting, bor-ing! But today, you're my project. Those people came to visit you and you're sitting there like a lump." Bernice sat in the visitor's chair and faced John. "What's the deal?"

"It's my daughter, Lizzie," John said. "You haven't met her. Her husband won't let her come to visit. He says he needs her to be with the kids and he doesn't want her upset, seeing me in hospice. I'd think it would upset her more not to be able to say good-bye."

"Doesn't she have any gumption? Girls nowadays. Hmph."

"She won't cross him. He's got a tight hand on the checkbook. He has a mistress and maybe a girlfriend besides. I had a detective check him out. I don't think Lizzie knows. I'm not sure if the mistress knows about the girlfriend but somebody else can tell her."

"Well then. What would you like to happen?" Bernice asked. "I have friends in low places, you know."

"I wish he'd just go up in a puff of smoke. Barring that, I guess Lizzie could bring the kids and move back home with Edith, although I'm not sure how that would work out. Edith's pretty particular."

"Well, look, it's time for my soap opera. Let's watch it and think bad thoughts about, umm, what's his name?"

"Arthur. Never Art or Artie, always Arthur. I hate Arthur. I hate soap operas too."

"Don't be a sourpuss. You can get a lot of good ideas from soaps. Crank up your bed where you can see better. Hush up and watch." Bernice raised the volume. "Looky at that. Beau is out at some fancy restaurant, and that ain't Mrs. Beau by a long shot. See, already I'm getting' an idea."

After the commercial break, Bernice said, "So can you spare about $150? Is there a fancy restaurant like we just seen Beau at where your daughter lives? I think you ought to get a gift for Lizzie and Artie. A nice meal out. What do you think?"

"I think he'd tell her he had to use it for a client dinner instead. Then he'd take his mistress there and leave Lizzie at home with the kids. That's what I think."

"That's exactly what I think too. So let's do it," Bernice said. "Just go with the flow, John, go with the flow."

*

When Ken picked Bernice up from her shift, she was grinning. He asked, "Good Pink day?"

She said, "You know, it's a Pink Rule. When you're feelin' down or in a bad mood, go do something for somebody else. It'll cheer you right up. So that's what I did. I'm going to do a Random Act of Kindness for John. He hasn't got much time left. You're going to help me. It'll be like the old days."

Ken was a little confused. "The old days? We retired. What do you want to do?"

"I want to go to dinner. We'll be dining out in style in Rocktown come Saturday night, so you'd better get your suit cleaned and pick out a tie. Not that hideous green thing either. We got a job to do. We're gonna go see Arthur and fix his wagon. Here's what I'm thinking." Bernice explained her idea to Ken.

*

Bernice got her best dress pressed and picked out her jewelry, got her hair and nails done too. On Saturday, she and Ken drove to Rocktown for dinner. Having made the reservations for Arthur and his friend as John's gift, she'd made sure her table would be next to theirs.

The evening was going well. The restaurant had soft lighting, attentive tuxedoed waiters and tableside preparation of Caesar salads and fancy desserts. Bernice ordered her favorite appetizer. "I know some people think shrimp cocktail is low class, but I do love that spicy sauce. Watch this," she said as she squeezed lemon on the shrimp. "Did you see the little fizz of lemon juice? My hands will smell like Pledge all evening. How's your steak? I could smell the sizzle before the waiter even got here."

"It's one of the best I've ever had," Ken replied. "Or maybe not, considering how you're plotting against Arthur. How do you think it's going?"

"Shhh, the girl's drinking champagne like it's water. It's only a matter of time before she gets her nerve up to say something to him or has to use the bathroom. Either one works for me. Oh, there it is, she just stood up. I'm on! Wish me luck." Bernice followed the short-skirted blonde into the restroom.

*

The girl at the mirror was using the corner of a paper towel to soak up tears before they could ruin her mascara.

"Get makeup in your eye, honey?" Bernice asked. "That hurts like a son of a gun. I do it all the time."

"I'm gearing up for a fight with my boyfriend," the girl said. "He's got somebody on the side. Besides his wife I mean. We'd never be able to eat at a place like this if he got divorced. She'd take everything. I can deal with a wife, but a girlfriend? I'm not sharing. But what if he gets mad and dumps me? Who would pay the rent and the bills? I got a two-carat tennis bracelet on layaway at the mall!"

"Well dear, it's like they say, are you better off with him or without him? That's something only you can decide. I had to make that decision myself once. I thought about it and I confronted him. It worked out okay." Bernice had practiced her story to perfection.

"What happened?"

"Well, I said to him, Ken, that's his name, Ken. I know about that blonde floozy you got. No offense dear but floozies are always blonde. Ken, you got to choose, her or me. He started to hem-haw around and I got mad. He shouldn't have hesitated, you know? We were having Bananas Foster for dessert, the one where they pour rum on some bananas and set them on fire at the table? Well I just grabbed that bottle of rum and poured it right over his head. Left him sitting there in a big puddle and went on home. Had the locks changed before he dried out. He came around after a day or two. It seems that when he went to the floozy's house to be consoled, she had some other guy there. Never had a problem after that. Sometimes you just gotta show them you mean business."

The girl thought for a moment and said, "I like it. I like bananas too. I'll do it. What have I got to lose? If Arthur doesn't see it my way, well, my boss has been looking lonely. He's pretty cute, too. Thanks, lady." And she went back to the table.

Bernice waited a minute and followed. Sure enough, the tableside prep was underway, the rum bottle sitting away from the flames of the gas burner. The whole restaurant heard when the girl made her ultimatum and Arthur, like Bernice had known he would, faltered. The girl stood up, grabbed the rum bottle and poured the contents over his head. His comb-over melted, and rum puddled in the pockets and creases of his pale-blue leisure suit. Without missing a step, the girl left the restaurant yelling, "You have to even think about it? Girlfriend or me, Arthur, you shouldn't need to think about it, girl-friend or me."

All the men looked anywhere but at Arthur or their women. The women looked at each other and smiled. Bernice jumped up and yelled at Ken. "I have to go feed the cat. You never worry about Snookums. It's always on me. I asked you one time to feed him and now you tell me you forgot? I have to go; he gets his medicine when he eats!"

As she rushed from the table, Bernice lost her footing and tripped against the burner holding the Bananas Foster. She tried to catch herself but burned her hand and knocked the waiter onto his butt. The burner pitched forward and landed in Arthur's lap, igniting the fumes of the rum, as a whoosh sound of flames filled the room.

As a kid, Arthur must not have seen the drop-and-roll movie, the one the fire department always shows at schools. He jumped up and tried to use the tablecloth to smother the flames. Unfortunately, the cloth was soaked with rum too and he only made matters worse. A fast-thinking busboy ran out with a fire extinguisher and aimed the nozzle at Arthur.

*

"Captain Lewis, we followed all the rules about tableside cooking. If the girl had not doused the man with rum, nothing would have happened. The stove turns off automatically after it tips over," said the manager. "I just hope we can get rid of the melted polyester smell before we reopen."

"It's unfortunate all around. The old guy said his wife has Alzheimer's and he wanted to give her a nice night out since she'd been doing so well. I guess she has that sundowner's thing. She thought she had to take care of the cat. He says the cat died of old age about twenty years ago. Anyway, my report says the restaurant is not at fault. If he hadn't been wearing polyester, it wouldn't have burned him so bad. If he hadn't been fooling around on her, the girl wouldn't have poured rum on him. Woulda liked to have seen that part. But I would advise teaching your people how to properly use a fire extinguisher. It was getting a lungful of the chemicals that killed him in the end."

*

Bernice and Ken drove home. "It was just like you said, worked like a charm. Bernice, we got away with it again. What a performance you gave! I miss the old days, don't you? And that was a nice touch about the cat."

Bernice looked at him, her face blank, "Cat? What cat?"

The Perfect Bite

"Now remember, don't overeat. The restaurant is very upscale. We'd be on the waiting list forever if someone hadn't canceled for tonight."

"You've told me about a hundred times now. Give it a rest, will you?"

"I just don't want to get on the bad side of the owners. I'd like to be able to eat here again."

"It'll be fine, you'll see. I *can* behave in public, you know."

Bert handed his car keys to the valet. A doorman ushered the two men inside.

"This *is* nice."

"I told you. That's why we have to be on our best behavior. This isn't the $3 all-you-can-eat early bird special. The menu is designed with the clientele in mind, from beginning to end."

The tuxedoed host led Bert and Sol to their table. Artfully folded red napkins stood in sharp relief against the dark brown tablecloths. The men were seated, napkins in lap, as the sommelier approached the table.

"Gentlemen, would you like a bottle of our best to start or would you rather choose your entrées first?"

"I'd love a glass now. What do you recommend?" Bert said.

As they discussed vintage, availability and the effect of the weather and environment on the end taste, Sol looked around. The restaurant was elegance itself, with subdued lighting that glowed from wall sconces. One wall was better lit and Sol saw the evening's specials highlighted there.

"Gentlemen, have you dined with us before?" Their server had only to glance at the busboy before a speck of lint was swept away.

"I have, but this is my friend's first time," said Bert. "I told him it will be like nothing he's ever had before."

"Welcome, sir. I assure you, the restaurant will measure up to your friend's recommendation. We do pride ourselves on impeccable service and the finest dining experience. May I direct your attention to the evening's menu?"

Bert and Sol turned to check out the listings. "Oh, I do love Mexican," said Sol. "I hope it's not too spicy though. Mild is about as daring as I can go."

"Then sir, you'll love this entrée. The chef has determined just which peppers, onions, and herbs combine to provide a bit of heat without overwhelming the more subtle flavors that Mexican cuisine offers. Shall I order it for you?"

"Yes, I think so. There are a number of items I'd love to have but Mexican appeals to me tonight. It's not often one can find upscale food instead of the usual Tex-Mex."

"Sir, have you decided or do you have any questions?"

Bert nodded. "I wanted to ask about the rustic dinner. What exactly is it?"

"The chef is very fond of mushrooms. Hen-of-the-woods, chanterelles and morels combine with forest grown ramps, and wild game. I believe you'd be very happy with that choice if you are in the mood for a robust flavor."

"It does sound like the perfect choice. Yes, please put in my order," said Bert. Looking at Sol, he added, "I never thought of myself as the rustic type, but I can't resist mushrooms and wild game. This is going to be the dining experience of a lifetime."

Conversation was hushed throughout the restaurant as diners concentrated on their meals. Soft music played in the background, loud enough to be heard but not enough to distract. Of course, no smoking was allowed.

"Will there be dessert? I forgot to ask," said Sol. "I do have a sweet tooth."

"The chef does like to provide a sweet to end the meal. I had a combination of raspberry and chocolate when I was here before," Bert said. "It was delicious, just enough to satisfy, but not enough to overwhelm the palate."

"It will be hard to go back to our usual fare after this. Genetically modified synthetics will suffer by comparison to the all-natural, organic menu choices here. We'll be spoiled."

"Gentlemen, your entrées are ready. Chef is only warming them to the optimum temperature to bring out the flavors to heighten your enjoyment. Allow me to refill your glasses during the short wait."

Sol asked, "Is this the only seating you have for tonight?"

"No sir, we have two seatings. Each has its own menu. Your friend chose this one based on the variety of items we anticipated for tonight. I hope that you find it all you hoped for."

"I'm completely happy so far. I would like to have a taste of something sweet..." Before Sol could continue, there was the loud sound of slurping and chewing coming from a table about six feet away. Instantly, waiters converged on the table, and pulled the unlucky diner from his seat. He fought and screamed, "More, I want more! I *need* more! Let me go, I have to have it..."

Servers and a large man, assumed to be a bouncer of sorts, escorted him out through the kitchen. Busboys raced to the table, collected the glassware and switched the stained tablecloth and napkins for a clean setup. In under a minute, there was no sign there'd been any trouble.

"Oh my, you weren't kidding about this place. Did you see that?" Sol didn't know what to make of the scene.

"I tried to tell you. I've never seen that happen before, but a friend of mine did and described it to me. He didn't do it justice." Bert tugged at his friend's sleeve. "Don't worry. When our food arrives, just go ahead and eat. I'm sure our server and busboys will keep an eye on us so we mind *our* manners at least. I'd hate to be the cause of a spectacle like that."

"My apologies, gentlemen. While we do admit our chef's food is beyond compare, sometimes a guest will lose all inhibition and overindulge. We feel this disrespects Chef and the establishment. There are strict rules in place to prevent this." Their server continued. "I'm sure Chef will come out to apologize as soon as everyone is served." He went back to the kitchen.

The meals arrived at the table moments later. All the disruption was forgotten as Bert and Sol took their first bites. "I can see why that man got so carried away," Sol said. "I've lived a long and varied life, but I've never had anything like this before."

"Is the amount of spice what you had in mind?" Between bites, Bert forced himself to sit back and take a look around the dining room. "I can taste all the subtle differences between the mushrooms. The game taste is there too, but it doesn't overwhelm the other flavors."

"It is exactly what I wanted. I do hope we're able to come back. This has been delightful. It's a wonder there's not a show about this on the Cooking Channel." He laughed and had to wipe his eyes. "They have every other kind of show you could imagine."

"Wouldn't that be something? People just wouldn't know what to make of it, so much attention to detail. They're used to fast food, grab a bite where you can, never mind the taste, just fill up on any old thing." Bert smiled too. "Oh look, the chef is making his rounds. I wonder if he'll remember me. No reason for him to, but it would be nice."

The chef wore the traditional checked pants and tall white toque. As he made his way to each table, servers introduced him to diners. Finally, he approached Sol and Bert. The busboy had just removed the entrées and refilled their glasses.

"Chef, allow me to introduce Mr. Bert, who was our guest last year for the brilliant holiday meal we served. This is his friend, Mr. Sol, who is dining with us for the first time."

"Ah, Mr. Bert, so nice to see you again. I remember how you enjoyed your meal. As they say, bacon makes everything taste better," Chef said as he shook Bert's hand. "Welcome, Mr. Sol. I hope you enjoyed your Mexican meal tonight."

"I did, Chef. I certainly can see why Bert has such

fond memories of his previous visit. I do hope we'll be able to come again." Sol also hoped the hint would rate them another meal without having to wait for a cancellation.

"But of course, Mr. Sol. Andre, be sure to give the gentlemen my card before they leave," said Chef. "When you call, tell the hostess the word written on the back of the card. She will take care of your reservations. As you know, we are booked almost two months in advance at all times. Now, because the ambiance of your dining experience was marred by the bad behavior of one of the guests, please allow me to send dessert to your table with my compliments." Chef bowed and returned to the kitchen.

"Gentlemen, tonight's sweet is a rich, dark chocolate, artfully blended with the sweetest, tiniest strawberries available."

The men found the dessert to be just as described. It was the perfect bite to end the meal.

"Thank you for inviting me, Bert."

"My pleasure, old friend. Here, let me help you with your coat."

The two men left the restaurant and decided to walk a bit before heading for home. "The grounds are just lovely." Bert appreciated the view.

"I can hear voices. What are they saying?" Sol took a few steps toward the rear of the building. The restaurant manager was issuing instructions to a number of men while handing out their pay for the evening.

"The thing you must do, is stick to the diet exactly. Phillippe, don't eat quite so many truffles. The flavor almost overwhelmed the roast goose taste. Carlos, great work. Just enough peppers, onions, and Mexican spices to bring out the best without being too hot. Jake, your diner loved the rustic taste. Will you be able to eat mushrooms and game again for the next meal?" One of the men nodded. "Excellent. Desserts, you were fabulous! Keep up the good work. Alex, can you stomach hot and spicy Chinese food? We have a request for the hotter, the better. Good! Remember that your blood accentuates even the most subtle flavors, so you must be careful not to eat too much of any one ingredient. Balancing flavors is the key."

He continued, "As you know, Ethan's diner over-indulged, but you'll be glad to know, everything is fine now. Remember, you are not allowed to work until fifty-six days from now. We keep strict records, so no trying to come back sooner. Now, please go home, recuperate, and rest."

The men were helped to waiting taxis by busboys.

Sol and Bert looked at each other. "What do you think?" Sol said.

"I think we'll be back in fifty-six days," said Bert, his fangs glistening in the moonlight. "Roast goose? Just don't let me overindulge."

Blue Moon

"Star light, star bright, first star I see tonight. I wish I may, I wish I might, have the wish I wish tonight."

"Whaddya gonna wish for, Pete?"

"Dunno, mebbe all the candy I can eat from McGregor's. Mebbe a whole nickel's worth."

"Don't be a dummy, you ain't ever even seen a nickel."

"Don't you be a dummy. That's why they call it a wish."

The boys moved on, pushing and shoving as they ran, dreaming of licorice whips, taffy, horehound bits, chewy caramels and lemon drops.

Bob knew better. A heart's desire doesn't come true by wishing on a star. It comes true when you have a definite goal and then work and plan to achieve it, no matter the cost.

While some might call Bob eccentric, some an odd-jobs man, Bob knew he was an inventor, a creator and maybe even a genius. He invented a lot of things—stories sometimes, his background, ways to fix and improve things, although, even he had to admit, the automatic chicken plucker hadn't been his best idea. However, Henrietta, the test chicken, had survived, although, she still held a grudge and tried to peck him whenever he came near. It didn't help that Henrietta belonged to Sam Larrane, the bank president. It made Sam loathe to loan Bob money for his inventions, even the bicycle-activated spit for roasting meat over a fire, or the strong magnets designed to hold a horse's shoes in place in lieu of nails. The blacksmith strongly objected to that one.

Bob did a lot of small jobs to make enough money to finance his inventions. One of the most tedious was going from farm to farm to teach youngsters who didn't see any reason why they should learn to read or write. Considering that some of them couldn't outthink a mule that pulled a plow, Bob couldn't come up with any reasons either.

Once a month, his rounds took him a day's travel away to Albersville where he had the good fortune to meet Sally Goodman, widow of the late Saul Goodman, recently deceased due to an infection from a bad cut on his leg. He'd been after a chicken destined for the Sunday dinner table and missed his mark—another case where the chicken won.

The Widow Goodman had two sons, Elias and Jonah, ages seven and nine, respectively. Both boys loved to learn. Bob found himself on the road to Albersville once a week instead of the once a month he was scheduled. Sometimes, he stayed overnight and slept in the barn. The breakfasts at the Goodman home were worth the bother of barn cats running over him in the dark as he counted sheep and they hunted mice.

Each time he arrived, the boys were excited to see what new books he brought and what tales he could tell about how other people lived in the world. He talked about what was out of the world too. Late into the evening, he'd point out stars and tell their names. He would describe the moon from sliver to full and back again in language that was almost poetic. When it was time for him to go, the boys often begged him to stay. It got harder and harder for Bob to leave.

Bob gave a lot of thought to the situation. He thought the Widow Goodman would be open to his request to court her when a suitable time period for mourning had passed, but what advantage could he offer? Surely other men would come calling, men of wealth and property, able to support the small family in a fine fashion.

The only thing to do then was to make enough money to give weight to his offer. The problem was *how* to make the money. Bob thought ideas should come to a genius like himself pretty readily, but for several months, he had to admit, he was stumped for a solution.

Things became more urgent when Sally's father

died and she moved back to her childhood home, three days' travel away. Bob felt his future slip through his fingers.

When two full moons occur during one calendar month, it's considered a good omen, or lucky by some. Bob wouldn't have been one of them except for three things. This was one of those months, Bob had an idea, and a stranger came to town. The three things converged. It was a once in a blue moon opportunity.

He first made the acquaintance of the stranger, a man without means nor relatives, a drunk when he could afford it, a beggar when he couldn't. Bob offered the man a small wage if he'd help build Bob's newest invention. The stranger quickly agreed and didn't even ask what was required of him or what the invention was. After all, he was thirsty.

A few evenings were spent with pencil and paper, sketches made, costs estimated, before Bob was ready to present his idea. Bob then went to the bank to call on Sam Larrane and inadvertently, Henrietta, who had accompanied Sam to work that day. The first obstacle was to get past Francis Wilson, guardian of the gate, also known as Sam's secretary. Of course, she had to know what business he had with the banker before she'd approve the visit, even though he could plainly see Sam at his big desk, half asleep in his big chair.

Anything told to Francis, and everything was,

turned into gossip, and gossip spread as fast as a wildfire in prairie grass. Francis was part of Bob's plan.

Once in Sam's office, Bob showed the drawings, explained his purpose, unsure if Sam would turn him down as he had so many times before, but to his surprise and delight, Sam was enthusiastic. He guaranteed half the money personally and the other half from the bank. Bob left, whistling a happy tune. He didn't hear Sam tell Henrietta, "This will be your revenge. We'll be rid of him once and for all." Henrietta clucked in agreement and had a smirk on her little chicken face.

Meanwhile, Bob put part three of his plan to work. When people asked him about his invention, he sold tickets so they could see it in action. He and the stranger began to build a giant catapult. Not only the children gathered around to watch, but adults often stopped to check the progress.

Bob spent a lot of time explaining what would happen when the mechanism was released. People shook their heads and scrounged enough money from the sale of crops or eggs to buy tickets to the big event. Their curiosity overcame their annoyance at Bob's air of superiority with all his book learning. Besides, the craziness he got up to was always good for a laugh.

At last the catapult was done and the launch was timed to coincide with the blue moon. For once, children willingly took their naps so they could stay up late and see Bob in all his glory. Three mules pulled the catapult to the launch site. Enterprising women cooked and sold food, the bartender iced a keg of beer, and the kids ran wild while attempts were made to catch fireflies.

The watchers had to stand back, and were glad to do so, since they'd seen Bob's inventions in action before. Sam and Henrietta were in the first row. The blacksmith stood nearby. The kids all sat on the ground and for once, sat still. With a great deal of showmanship, Bob mounted a small platform and began his speech. Most wished he'd just get on with the program.

"Citizens of Cedarwood, friends, students and supporters, I come before you tonight with my greatest invention yet. What stands here, my own design, built with the help of my assistant," Bob waved to the stranger who took an unsteady bow, "is a catapult of immense power and magnitude that can work on one night and one night only, the night of the blue moon. It is neither to launch a defense as in olden times nor simply to entertain. My friends, what is to be launched, is in fact, me."

The crowd gasped. Only Sam Larrane had known the purpose of Bob's invention. He didn't understand how it would work, or even if it would, but if it were possible, it was worth every penny.

"Yes, my good folks, I've studied the skies and

have designed the machine that will carry me to the stars and beyond. This catapult is strong enough to propel me to the moon."

One of the women fainted, two children who'd fallen asleep were poked and prodded by brothers and sisters until they woke, and the men muttered comments that questioned Bob's sanity, paternity and common good sense as related to what God gave a goose.

"My assistant and I will now adjourn to the launch site and prepare for my journey. I wish you prosperity and happiness for all your days. I am certain I shall achieve the same."

With that, Bob and the stranger walked into the distance and soon people could see the silhouette of one boosting the other into a seat on the catapult. A great creaking sound moaned low over the quiet crowd as the catapult was stretched further back. A twang and whistling made children cover their ears, and adults strained to see as the trigger was released.

The silhouette of a man sailed through the air until he was lost from sight. A sigh was the only sound heard until one man said, "Nothing more to see. Let's head home and get the young'uns to bed."

*

Neither Bob nor the stranger was ever seen again. The catapult remained in place until the children got too curious; then the adults dismantled it, destined for the wood pile.

At bedtime, a child would sometimes stare out the window and ask, "Mama, is there really a man in the moon?"

The answer was always the same. "Yes, dear, his name is Bob."

*

In Jessup's Gap, Bob sat on the back porch with Elias and Jonah while Sally cleared the dinner table. He pointed out the stars and told their names. He described the moon from sliver to full and back again in language that was almost poetic.

He'd wished happiness and prosperity to his friends and neighbors in Cedarwood. He'd found his own happiness with Sally. As for prosperity, the ticket sales and money he'd saved by not paying his assistant, ensured their future. He'd given the man just enough cash to allow him to get drunk, then put him into the seat of the catapult and flung him into the deserted area outside of town. Only the coyotes and buzzards were interested to see where he landed.

Elias asked, "Is there really a man in the moon?"

"No," said Bob. "That's just a story created by an inventive mind."

Sweet Tea and Deviled Eggs

The minister was droning on about Miz Ethel's many virtues and none of her sins. In spite of the 90-degree temperature, he didn't show any sign of letting up. At least he'd known her personally, not like some ministers who will give a canned eulogy for just anybody. I rubbed the sore spot on my arm and let my mind drift, back to when the dying began.

I'd never seen a "real live" dead body before—even TV didn't show many bodies in those days. Perry Mason would defend a murderer and we'd see the corpse, shot once or knocked over the head. It was nothing like today's shows when you get to see the body's insides handed from one person to another as they find the means, motive and killer in less than an hour. Not all crimes are that easy to figure out.

My Daddy was the first to die—not ever, of course, but the first person I knew who up and died before they got really old or sick. They said it was because he drank so much for so long. That night he drank up all the beer from the fridge, got up off the couch and headed to the basement for more. In my mind, I see him tripping over his own feet, falling down the steps. Momma found him in the morning. She was sleeping pretty heavy due to the medicine she was taking, so hadn't heard him fall. The doctor, who doubled as the coroner, said it probably wouldn't have made any difference. Daddy'd been too drunk to know he was dying.

The funeral was kinda nice over all. We had to go for the plainest casket, but a lot of people showed up. I think some wanted to make sure Daddy was really dead, and some were just being nosy. Most came because of Momma.

She looked real pretty in the first new dress she'd had in years. Daddy was tight with money, except for buying beer. He told her, "You never go anywhere, what do you need with a new dress?" and she'd get real quiet. If I said anything to her, she'd just give me a big hug and say, "Your Daddy has his own demons. Let him be." But she looked real sad to me.

Things got better for us after Daddy died. I guess you shouldn't be glad someone's gone, but facts are facts, we were better off. Daddy had insurance from his job so we had living-on money. And most important at the time, we still had health insurance. Momma was happier, but still not well.

She went out more that fall, loved seeing the leaves turn all the colors. She came to parent-teacher nights at school, wearing a new dress with her hair all done up nice. Once in a while, some man would ask her out to dinner, but she always said no. "I've had enough of a man's company, it's time to enjoy my own," she'd say. They'd look puzzled, but learned not to ask twice.

Thanksgiving was a big deal that year. She said we had so much to be thankful for. She made a turkey, the cranberries I love, sweet potatoes, and let me eat all the dressing I wanted. My stomach hurt all night but I didn't regret it.

Christmas was even better. Momma was able to shop. She spent a lot of time getting just the right thing for each person on her list. The night we wrapped presents is clear in my mind. Red and green paper all over the floor, and we lost the scissors and tape, I don't know how many times. Every package had to have a big bow and a nametag. Our tree was six feet tall and the star almost touched the ceiling. Momma bought little red apple ornaments to hang on it, tied a million red gingham bows, and used white lace hankies she'd bought at the Goodwill as ornaments. We invited everybody over and ate cookies and drank eggnog until we couldn't hold any more.

I'm glad we had that time because after Christmas, Momma got sicker, and before summer, she died. I was thirteen years old, and an orphan.

Momma wasn't the second dead person I'd seen

though. That was Mr. Don, Miz Ethel's husband. I didn't like Mr. Don. Miz Ethel would wear long sleeves in the summertime or stay in the house for a week at a time. Once in a while, I'd see the bruises, but pretended not to so she wouldn't be embarrassed. Now and again, it would be bad enough we could hear her cries over at our house.

Mr. Don died right before Easter. We were having warmer days but cool nights then. Miz Ethel had fixed a whole dozen deviled eggs and a big pitcher of sweet tea and planned to share them with us. Mr. Don didn't approve of sharing. He hit Miz Ethel so hard, she had to go to her sister's house and get May Belle to take her to Doc to get her arm fixed up. Miz Ethel stayed at May Belle's. Mr. Don just went on to work.

When he got home, Mr. Don ate every last one of those deviled eggs. Doc figured they disagreed with him and he went to bed sick. He must have had chills during the night, because they found him under the electric blanket, it turned up on high. He'd been dead for three days, just like Jesus in the Easter story, except Mr. Don didn't rise up again.

Miz Ethel didn't seem to mind that Mr. Don had died in the house. She went right back there after the funeral and stayed. She was a big help when Momma got so sick, and when Momma died, Miz Ethel had me move into her house. At first, I thought Mr. Don might come back and haunt me, but after a few months, I was able to sleep through the night again, no more lying awake and waiting.

Miz Ethel had asked me once, in a roundabout way, about the night my Daddy fell down the basement steps. I understood her to say, she thought Momma had pushed him and didn't blame her one bit. I didn't say anything, but I just knew that wasn't true.

It seems like I always knew Momma was sick and wouldn't be with me for all my growing up. And she didn't want to leave me with Daddy, drunk as he was all the time. Sooner or later, he'd lose his job, we'd get kicked out of the rent house and then where would I be?

So I thought it best to handle things myself.

Daddy liked to sit in front of the TV and drink once he got home from work. We had one shelf in the fridge, just for beer. We kept more in the basement, where it was nice and cool. I made my plans, and I must say, it all went very smoothly.

Momma and I had hot chocolate with marshmallows every night before bed. I slipped one of her sleeping pills in her cup, as I did when I thought she looked too tired, and she slept like a baby, right through the night.

After school, I'd moved most of the beer from the fridge down to the basement. I knew the half-dozen I'd left in the fridge wouldn't last long. Sure enough, I heard Daddy go to the kitchen and then start cussing because the shelf was empty. I heard him bump the table and kick a chair as he went to the basement door. The door creaked so I knew just when he opened it and started down the steps. And I heard him when he fell.

He laid at the bottom of the steps and moaned, called out for help and then cussed because nobody came. I went to the door and looked down at him. Poor Daddy, his demons had gotten him but good.

I stepped carefully, bent down and removed the thin wire I'd stretched over the third step down. Daddy had never even noticed it. Winding it around my fingers, into a little ball, I sat on the steps until Daddy got quiet. Then I went to bed. I had a big math test the next day. As I recall, I did real well on it.

Of course if Momma's sickness took her, I'd need a place to live. The obvious choice was Miz Ethel. Except, there was Mr. Don. I just couldn't bring myself to live in the same house with him. So I made another plan.

The day Miz Ethel made the deviled eggs, the plan for Mr. Don went just as smooth as the plan for Daddy had. With Miz Ethel out of the house nobody could blame her for what happened next. After Mr. Don left for work, I went over to their house and let myself in. It didn't take but a few minutes to get the sample pain pills Doc used to give Miz Ethel and smash them up. I took the yolks out of the eggs and mixed the pills in, then refilled the eggs. Mr. Don ate like a pig; he wouldn't notice any funny taste.

It didn't take long for the pills to act. He got woozy and headed for bed. He was too dizzy to even get undressed, for which I was very thankful, and fell on the bed still in his red plaid flannel shirt and brown corduroy pants. I waited a few minutes, and when he didn't move, set the scene. I brought in his glass of sweet tea and pressed it in his hand, let it drop and spill. I put all the little pill packages on the nightstand so it would look like Mr. Don took them himself. And then I covered him with the electric blanket, turned it up on high and went on home.

"How did you know Ethel?" The voice startled me and I jumped. "Sorry, I didn't mean to sneak up on you. I was just asking, how did you know Ethel? I know her from St. John's Church. I'm Lila, by the way."

The minister had finally finished talking and people were starting to move toward their cars. "I lived next door to Ethel. She was a very kind woman."

"Dear, you've got to be so hot in those long sleeves! It must have been over 90 today. Will you be coming back to the church? We're gathering in the basement, sharing a little food and, I hope, talking about our memories of Ethel. It isn't far from here."

I absently rubbed the sore spot on my arm. "No, I don't think I can. I have to get home and fix my husband's supper. He's very particular about it being on time. He'll wonder where I've got to."

"It would be nice if men ate salad, wouldn't it? But no, they are all like my Ed, they want a hot meal, even if it steams up the whole kitchen. What are you going to make, dear?"

"I was just thinking—I think I'll make a big pitcher of sweet tea and some deviled eggs. He deserves that."

www.ingramcontent.com/pod-product-compliance
Lightning Source LLC
Chambersburg PA
CBHW061549310726
48972CB00008B/2678